OMG UR A TEENAGER

LESLIE E. YOUNG

North Carolina

Published in the United States by BQB Publishing
(an imprint of Boutique of Quality Books Publishing Company)
www.bqbpublishing.com

ISBN: 979-8-88633-029-8 (p)
ISBN: 979-8-88633-030-4 (e)

Library of Congress Control Number: 2024934495

Book design by Robin Krauss, www.bookformatters.com
Cover design by Rebecca Lown, www.rebeccalowndesigns.com

Editor: Allison Itterly

Chapter 1

"I got it!" Jen flew through my bedroom door.

"What?" I asked. "What did you get?"

My bestie sidled up beside me and smiled. "You know . . . what we've been talking about."

"A boyfriend?" I giggled.

"I wish." She waved me on. "Go again."

"Uh . . . um . . ." I flopped down on my bed and gazed up at her, clueless.

"*Duh!* Kat, I got my period."

"Period? What's that?" a voice squeaked from my door.

My seven-year-old brother Max swooped in, superhero-style. His Spider-Man wings, cut from an old badminton net, spread wide to look like webs. He zoomed around the room, angling his wings to ensnare my desk chair and toppling a pile of magazines to the floor before skittering back to the door. My bratty brother always found a way to stick in his two cents.

"Get out of my room!" I hollered.

"I'm not in your room." He poked out his tongue at me.

I quickly scurried Max all the way out and shut the door in his face. His footsteps pounded down the hallway, running to Mom, of course. Fine with me.

My parents' gym, Cruz's Athletic Club, hadn't recovered after Silver's Gym swept into the neighborhood and bit off a whole chunk of our regulars. Silver's Gym was shiny and new with oodles of space for more equipment and classes, a basketball court, and even a swimming pool. Membership at our plain old gym slumped, and my parents had to lay off some employees. Dad was working at the gym nonstop. Mom was working there longer and longer hours, and I was stuck with Max. *A TON*.

Max's superhero-fantasy life snowballed and my tween social life crashed. Seriously, I had almost no personal life. My friends were literally forced to come to *me* for urgent, in-the-flesh face time.

Thank God for my bestest pal, Jen. She lived in the same apartment building and popped in all the time.

"Sorry about the Spider-Man blitz," I told her. I leaned back against my Barbie-pink headboard and cuddled my raggedy old Sleeping Beauty doll that still hung out on my bed.

"So, I'm dying to hear what happened."

"Well," she said, settling down in my desk chair and leaning in. "First, I had some cramping." She let out a deflated sigh. "Ugh. Totally sucky."

"Ouch," I groaned.

"Then I felt something wet in my pants." She scrunched up her nose. "So gross."

"Eww."

The truth? I wanted my period with all my heart. Yeah, it sounded awful. But it was the price we women paid to cross the bridge from childhood to adulthood. Jen had hers. I wanted to be next. Maybe then Mom would start treating me like the almost-teenager I was instead of the child that I was not.

Jen slouched down and raked her fingers through her carroty-red pixie. Then her green eyes lit up. "That's not all." She pulled up her T-shirt and stuck out her chest, showing off her new B-cup bra. It was Fourth-of-July themed, with red, white, and blue flags scattered all over.

"There's more. Check it out." She hopped

up and pulled down her baggy boyfriend jeans just enough for the total reveal. "The matching panties!"

So lucky. No boyfriend yet, but the big P and a new bra.

For forever, we'd been practically identical in some ways. We were both five-three-ish, one-hundred-pound sixth graders at Grant Middle School. Then, all of a sudden, Jen had a growth spurt, shot up two-plus inches, added ten pounds—and curves. Now, one glimpse in a mirror punched out a whole different pic of us, with Jen all shapely lines and me a stick figure. Super awkward for me. To be honest, I felt a twinge of envy.

Figures, though. Jen actually started blossoming last summer, but my chest was still as flat as a board. I'd gone with her for her first fitting of an AA-cupper, so I totally knew how to get the straps and cups just right. When my time came for my bra fitting, I'd be ready. But worse luck, any growth spurt in me seemed pitifully slow. I was twelve going on thirteen, so I hoped my growth spurt would happen soon.

Turning thirteen, more than getting a bra or my period, was of course the absolute towering milestone I had my heart set on, when I would get all the recognition and privilege of teenhood. I imagined I would then feel just like Sleeping Beauty awakening or Cinderella transforming from a scullery maid into a princess.

I was deep in thought when the door whooshed wide open. Jen and I yanked our heads around. Mom and Max stood there, saucer-eyed. Jen covered her flags, and I sucked in a deep breath.

"Ever hear of knocking?" I asked as patiently as I could.

Mom shot me her frowniest look. "Max wants to know when he'll get his period," she said, all breathless. She flashed me a look that said: *I need an answer, and it better be good.*

I rolled my eyes, my signature response for *Fine. Whatev.*

Max propped his spider-web arms on his non-hips.

Mom pinched her lips. "Why did he ask?"

I raised a brow. "I dunno."

She squeezed her eyes shut as if she'd mustered her last shred of patience. Her voice grew screechy. "He's seven!"

Max was still playing the baby card like it was

a get-out-of-jail-free pass. So, to throw some shade on his tattling, I launched my defense. I arched my eyebrows and made one of those throat-clearing *ahem* sounds to turn the full spotlight on my case. Then I dramatically tossed my inky-black curls behind me and narrowed my dark eyes on Mom.

"Well," I said, "I'm *almost* a teenager. And, FYI, someone *did* get her period!"

Now Mom has to notice I am on the threshold of womanhood. And Max is a meddler.

Mom lowered her glasses, considering. "Who got her period?"

Jen grinned.

Mom blinked as the truth blazed into sight. "Ooooooh," she said. She pushed her glasses back up. "Max, stay out of Kat's room." She turned to me. "Stop being so mean to your little brother. And—"

She raved on, chewing me out as if I were a child. *As if.* I tuned her out.

Finally, I was saved by the ringing of the phone. Mom jumped at the sound. Worry lines cut between her eyes. "Probably Gran again," she muttered.

I loved my gran, but lately she'd been calling

about a lot of silly stuff. Yesterday, it was how to set a table, even though I'd seen her do it just fine a jillion times before.

Mom turned her crinkled brow on Max. "Honey," she said in a syrupy-sweet voice. "Go play with your marbles while Mommy talks to Gran." She flashed her worry frown at me and sighed. Then she stomped out of the room, dragging Max with her.

Really, there is no justice in this family.

Soon after, Jen went home to change her pad. When would my period come? Would I ever wear a bra? I wasn't shooting for a Wonder Woman miracle. Any cup size would do.

I pasted two Post-its on my bulletin board, the one above my laptop desk that screamed "For Girls Only" with its pink, scalloped border and T-W-E-E-N written in huge pink letters. I scribbled a note reminding me to ask Mom about buying me a bra. It wasn't like I was asking for the moon or anything. I pinned up one more note written in marker and all caps: KEEP MAX OUT.

Not even an hour later, Mom rapped on my door.

"Off to work in a few," she called out. "Keep an eye on Max."

"Again?" I moaned. I knew my parents had to work, but babysitting five times a week—*five times*—was a real pain.

"I heard that," Mom sang, throwing open my door and pushing her yucky veggie smoothie at me, her latest inedible health drink mixed with dandelions.

"*Blech.*" I wrinkled my nose and shot out my hand to cut her off.

Mom chuckled. She swished her long dark hair behind her and paraded out the door.

I headed into the living room. Our time-worn sofa had been sat on and scrubbed clean so many times that a throw cover was permanently draped over it to hide the worst spots on the cushions. On the coffee table, a pile of magazines hid the stains that glasses and bottles had left behind. The rest of the table was littered with a bunch of unpaid bills from Walmart, Target, you name it.

Max crouched on the floor at the edge of a cardboard playing field with his marbles. A Superman T-shirt had replaced his Spider-Man netting. It didn't matter that he couldn't fly or spin a single web, he thought he was a hero.

I plopped down on the couch and worked on my article for the *Grantline Newsletter*. I'd just been named editor, not to toot my own horn or anything. I had been hooked on journalism ever since I was eight and had written my first story about saving polar bears for a school project. I had big dreams of writing for a newspaper.

Max was still engrossed in his game as marbles skipped from his fingertips and flew everywhere. I watched him out of the corner of my eye, wondering if a person could disown a sibling.

Clearly, the apartment we lived in was shrinking. Since Max was born, we had been busting out of our two-bedroom, plus a den that'd been transformed into a third bedroom. Max's so-called "bedroom" had no door or closet, just a small daybed and a few shelves for his clothes. No matter how often Mom neatly folded and placed his pants with his pants and shirts with his shirts, they always ended up a sloppy mishmash of everything all over the place.

Plus, his toys never seemed to return to their home in the basket under his bed, especially his beloved marbles. You were lucky if you could make it from the front door through the living room without stumbling over one of his stupid marbles. And Max never tired of blasting off his homemade toy space shuttle from the living room to the planet Krypton, where he was sure all the lost bits and pieces could be found.

Even worse than his stuff overflowing into every nook of our apartment was Max's latest habit of hanging out in my room and fiddling with my laptop. The situation was growing more annoying by the day, and I wasn't the only one who realized space was tight. Mom was all over Dad about it the minute he filed through the door later that night.

"Kat and Max got into it again today," Mom said.

I was relaxing on the couch, flipping through my *Girls' Life* mag, when I heard my name. It was impossible not to eavesdrop.

"What was it this time?" Dad asked. He sounded tired after a long day at the gym and barely concerned.

"Max went to use Kat's laptop and walked in on a *personal* conversation."

Dad shrugged. "Doesn't sound like such a big deal."

"Not a big deal?" echoed Mom.

She trailed him into the kitchen and her voice faded. I could hardly make out what she was saying about Max being in school now and needing a proper desk. I drifted toward the kitchen to find out.

"He's in first grade." Dad chuckled. He pulled a soda can from the fridge, popped it open, and gulped.

Mom got that tight-lipped look on her face. "We need more space, Sam," she said.

A long minute passed, and I was beginning to see that my privacy and Max's desk were sides of the main event. My parents had been "saving pennies" for a house since I could remember. They'd always opted to wait until they had the money to make a good move.

All the same, Mom went in for the kill with a brand-new slant to boost her case. "You know, moving to a home in a better neighborhood could open us up to a whole new clientele for the gym."

Dad's face lit up. Not much meant more to him than saving the family biz. "Good point, Dot," he said.

Then Mom stopped beating around any

bushes and said what she really wanted—a house, and there was no stopping her. They went back and forth about it, zigzagged this way and that, snaked here and there and all around it until Dad said, "Let's consider it."

As far as I knew, we hadn't won any lottery. So, what were they thinking? *Beats me.*

Chapter 2

The next weekend, we all went looking for a new home. Right away we hit the obvious snag. We couldn't afford practically anything. At the end of our search, the frontrunner was a house the bank had taken over after the owners couldn't pay for it.

Dad said we'd "lucked out." But when we drove up to the run-down place late Sunday afternoon, all we could do was stare. The porch steps were cracked, the front door hung lopsided off its hinges, and drab gray paint was peeling everywhere.

"Are you sure it's the right house?" Mom asked.

Dad pulled a piece of paper from his pocket. "Yeah. Thirteen Crystal Drive."

My heart sank. "It's gross."

And it had the unluckiest number of all pinned on it. Everyone knew Friday the thirteenth was *not* a good omen. The thirteenth floor was missing in tall buildings. Sports teams excluded the number from their rosters. The red flag could not have been clearer. It was like a warning from God to back off.

My dad did not pick up on this. He tilted his head to one side. "Needs a few cosmetic fixes on the outside." He winked, then pushed us toward the door. "Bet it's top-of-the-line in there."

I flinched. *Yeah right.* I wasn't the only doubtful one. Mom crunched her forehead. Even Max made a face. Still, we carefully maneuvered our way inside to find out.

"Look." Max laughed and pointed at a big empty space in the hall bathroom. "No toilet."

"Hey, matching empty spaces in here," I called out. The fridge and stove were missing in the grimy kitchen, where I tracked a cockroach shimmying up the wall until it vanished into a crack, no doubt heading for some feeding ground judging by the nauseating stink of dead things that wafted throughout the house. In the living room, dust balls were everywhere, and someone had scribbled on the wall in red marker as if warning us, *Buyer beware.*

"Could use a vacuuming," Mom said.

We took the full tour.

The minute we hit the second floor, Max was on the move. He was impressed that all four bedrooms had doors and closets and was ready to claim his. Tough choice, though. They were all in different states of ruin. One dark and dreary room had its only window boarded up, another had peeling wallpaper with massive pink roses all over it, and a third had a crack in one wall so large that it was hard to see how the room was standing. The fourth bedroom looked the best, but that was the master for Mom and Dad. No way was Max going to snag that one.

We trooped outside to the back of the house. It had a pretty decent-sized yard, but it was full of discarded junk: a beat-up dresser with half of its drawers missing, a wheelbarrow minus its wheel, and a rusted bike without its chain.

Yeah, the place was bigger than our apartment. *Big deal.*

Still, my mom thought it was fabulous—in a good neighborhood, close to the gym, not too far from my school. "Okay," she admitted. "It needs work."

"It's a fixer-upper," said Dad, smiling.

I gave them both a long look. "Whatever you call it, it's a total embarrassment!" There was no way I could tell anyone at school where I lived ever again. I wasn't even sure I wanted Jen to see it.

"Calm down, Kat," Mom said. "We'll make it work."

I stared at them in amazement. "You really want to do more work?"

No one answered.

There was nothing left for me to say, so I cut out of there.

I stood in front of the house, considering. The dream was to live in a bougie McMansion with a wow factor to drool over. This stinky place was the anti-dream times infinity, a creepy spookshow. I couldn't live in it. I couldn't.

Freaking out that I might have to, I turned my back on the house and gazed off in the distance at the Sandia Mountains that flanked the east side of Albuquerque. I marveled at the beauty of all the shades of pink that decorated the mountains at sunset. But the sun setting on the Sandias could not turn an ugly house beautiful. So I headed out to the car and waited for my family to catch up.

It was a sucky day. I didn't think anything could have made it worse until I saw Maria

Cudsupa, the biggest gossip at my school. She flew by on her bike, spotted me, and skidded to a stop. Her nose tipped high in the air as she flicked a dark bush of curly hair behind her. Taking her time, she blew a few loose flyaways from her forehead. Then she leaned over her handlebars and leveled her cold, gray eyes at me. "Is *that* your house?"

My cheeks burned. I bit my lip and searched for a good answer. My mom, dad, and blabbermouth brother were coming up behind me. I had nowhere to run, so I slapped on a smile. "Not yet," I said. Then I shrugged and casually examined my nails.

"*Mm-hmm.*" Maria tugged a stick of gum from the pocket of her jeans and shoved it into her mouth. She chomped smugly. "That your new pet?"

My eyes nearly popped out of my head when I saw Max dangling a dead rat by its tail. "*Ick!*" I shrieked.

Max grinned. He lifted the yucky thing up and thrust it forward for closer viewing.

"Throw that disgusting *thing* in the trash," Mom said, shuddering.

Maria cracked her gum and let out a wicked

cackle. Then she took off. "See ya in school," she hollered over her shoulder.

We piled into our SUV, which was as old as me and made horrible rattling noises. Clackety-clack-clack. *Another embarrassment.* As we drove off, clattering away, I swiveled around to check out the rattrap one more time and caught a glimpse of Maria. She was back at the house snapping a photo on her phone. My stomach plunged, doing a bazillion somersaults until I thought I might puke. *OMG. It's been docu-mented.* And Maria was the type of person who would spread it around. I blinked back tears and dreaded school the next day.

Mom looked at me with a sad little smile. "Everything will be fine, Kat."

I shrugged her off. At home, I hid out in my room and huddled under the covers. I kept checking Maria's Instagram to see if she'd posted anything, but there was nothing. *Thank God.*

If Mom and Dad persisted with this disastrous plan to relocate to a rat house, I might be forced to disown my whole family. Where would I live, though? I was stuck.

Chapter 3

After the worst Sunday of my life, I had to go to school and face Maria. I was not looking forward to it. I just hoped that she would ignore me and not say anything about the house.

Mom was on the phone with Gran again, answering some dopey question about how long to boil an egg. Dad was browsing Zillow for more houses. Max was chugging OJ at the kitchen table, and I was just moping.

I hadn't told Jen anything about the potential move. I hoped—prayed—that Mom and Dad would drop this crazy house idea. Instead, Dad told me they were on the way to the bank to strike a deal.

"When can we move?" Max asked, all amped up for a room of his own.

"When we sign on the bottom line of a contract with the bank," Dad said in a chipper voice.

Ugh. Their chatter was a double downer. I slung my backpack over my shoulder and headed outside. Jen was waiting for me near the curb like she always did. I dragged my feet all the way to school. I thought about cutting class, maybe hanging out at the mall. *Forever*.

Jen kept tossing me side glances. "What's with you?" she asked.

I let out a long sigh. "We're moving to a house."

She pitched her head to the side. "Wow, really? Isn't that good? Didn't you want more space?"

I froze to a dead halt. "It's not good. It's *terrible!* I *did* want space. But . . ."

"What?"

I sniffled. "My parents just went off to buy a wreck of a house that I wouldn't even want my dog to live in, and there's nothing I can do about it." I swallowed hard, refusing to cry and make my eyes all red on the way to school.

"Maybe they won't get it," Jen said in a positive way.

I sucked in a deep breath and let it out slowly. "I don't think there are any other takers. It's a dump. You have to bypass crumbling steps and a busted door to even get inside."

We both went quiet for a bit. Then Jen swung

her arm around my shoulder, and we trudged on.

"Hey. We're still on for Just Dance after school, right?" Jen smiled.

"Yeah," I mumbled.

Jen had been coming with me to my favorite exercise class at my parents' gym. Just Dance was a chill mix of hip-hop, jazz, and salsa. Today we were going to start a new routine to Ava Max's "Tattoo," and our dance instructor told us that we needed to bring our own stick-on tattoos. Jen was psyched about it. I was, too, before the bombshell that we would move into the house.

When we got to school, the warning bell was ringing.

"Later," Jen said, squeezing my arm.

I tossed her a half-hearted smile.

She disappeared into a swell of students, and I weaved through the crowd to head for homeroom. My steps slowed to a crawl. Maria *just happened* to be lingering near my locker.

"Moving into your new home?" she asked as a fake smile spread across her face.

"Undecided," I said. I brushed by and turned

my back on her, twirled my locker combo, and
fidgeted with some books.

"You'll let me know about the housewarm-
ing?" she said. "Kay?"

My fingers curled tight around one of my
books. I wanted to throw it at her.

"Def," I said close-lipped.

Maria did her witchy cackle and shuffled off.

I gritted my teeth and slammed my locker
shut. Ever since the third grade, Maria had been
picking on me. It all started because of the Glue
Incident. Maria and I had been paired up for a
school project. We'd gotten along just fine back
then and were working well together to create a
poster board of all the US states. She and I had cut
out all the shapes. She painted each individual
state, and I wrote detailed descriptions of each
state.

In a horrible turn of events, when I went to
paste the states to the poster board, the cap on
the glue bottle hadn't been secured properly and
a glob of glue spilled out all over the East Coast.
"I'm sorry, I'm sorry," I'd said. In haste, I tried
to wipe the glue off with a paper towel, but the
states all stuck together, and the glue mixing
with the paint created an ugly mess.

"Look what you did!" Maria had shouted.

But that wasn't even the worst part. Not only did I ruin Maria's perfectly painted states, but Chip had walked by at that exact moment and laughed at us.

Of course, Maria was upset and blamed me for ruining her life. Once we hit the sixth grade, Maria became cool and started hanging out with the seventh graders. She and her friends ruled the school. No one ever dared to stand up to them. I thought she really just enjoyed trying to make my life miserable.

So, Maria strolled through the door first before I slipped into class. Yep, same homeroom, Cruz and Cudsupa, alphabetically linked for life at Grant Middle School. *Cringe.*

As I drifted over to my seat, my classmates stared at me and whispered in a hushed, gossipy way. Or was it just my imagination? Had I gotten my period? Did I have blood on my jeans? I ran my hand over my pants and even snuck a peek. Nothing.

Then I noticed Maria smirking as she showed a girl something on her phone. I carefully slid out my iPhone and scrolled through Instagram, my finger swiping up the screen in a fury until I found

Maria's photo. The crumbling steps, the un-hinged door, peeling paint, even a rat—she'd caught it all. It already had 102 likes and counting. There were thirteen comments and counting. Nasty things like: *What a dump. Tacky place.* And, the worst, *Rathole.*

The boys behind me were giggling.

"Kat's new house is like a litter box," someone teased.

My face went red hot with humiliation. I shrank low in my chair and stared at my desk, but I could still feel my classmates' eyes boring into me. I squeezed my eyes shut and slid even lower in my chair, but I couldn't block out their laughs. Then I imagined Maria's smug smile pinned on me, and I could hardly breathe. When the homeroom period ended, I stayed glued to my seat, not caring if I ever made it to my next class, just determined not to walk the halls with Maria or any of the other classroom bullies.

———————

After the longest school day in history, I slogged over to the gym. Mom was at the sign-in desk talking about schedules with some members. I gave her a half-wave, then passed the long row of treadmill and Stairmaster machines to my right and my dad in a weight training session to my left. I trudged into Studio Room A for my Just Dance class with exactly zero enthusiasm.

My heart just wasn't into it today. I didn't even bother to paste on a tattoo, and my steps had no zing to them.

Worse, my head wasn't into it. I lost my focus, tripped over my own two feet while performing a simple jazz square, and tumbled to the floor. The music stopped. Everyone gawked. My face burned, and I just hung there for a long humiliating second until Jen reached out a hand and tugged me up.

"Are you okay?" asked the instructor.

All I could do was nod and move to the back of the room to finish the routine with more of a walk-through of steps than an actual dance.

"What's wrong?" Jen asked after class.

"The house and Maria," I said with a face full of gloom, then made a speedy exit to avoid blubbering about it in front of everyone.

Finally at home, I unloaded on my parents. First, I pulled up Maria's photos on my phone. Then I begged them, "*Pleeeeeease*, if you value your daughter's reputation, squash this ugly house idea."

"Well, the bank is considering our offer," Mom said.

"Knock on wood," Dad said with a twinkle in his eye. "The fixer-upper will be ours."

My insides turned over. Tears welled up in my eyes.

Mom made a feeble attempt to soften the blow. "We'll post a photo of the renovation on Facebook when it's done," she said as if that solved the problem.

IT DID NOT.

The tears leaked from my eyes and slipped down my cheeks.

The *only* good thing was that school was out for the summer at the end of the week. Was it possible that everyone would forget about our rathole by the time school started again? I was so looking forward to being in seventh grade. All I could do was hope.

Chapter 4

"Let the renovation begin," Dad said three weeks later, and that was the end of summer vacation as I knew it. No more fun or games, and almost no hanging out with Jen. *Nope*. Now everything was about the house reno. An inspector had found the house "sound," so we only had a few weeks to fix up the place and move in before school started.

My parents had hired some pros to rehang the front door, reconstruct the porch steps, and rehab the rickety railings. Fumigators wiped out the foul stench of rotting garbage and took care of the pest control—rats, roaches, ants, termites, and only God knows what else.

We had to replace the missing fridge, stove, and toilet, scrub the place clean, and paint. We hit every clearance sale around town for the absolute rock-bottom prices on appliances. We stocked up on huge amounts of cleaning supplies to scrub off the grime and wash down the place. And we took on the massive outside paint job—the prep, the spray-painting, and the trim. Plus, we had to clean out and pack up our whole apartment. So, the summer rolled by slowly in a continuous grind of dull drudgery.

We were down to painting touch-ups and trim when Max got really antsy about his bedroom. He'd picked his room last month when we settled on the house. He was afraid of the room with the big crack and refused to live in the room with the pink-flowered wallpaper. That left the gloomy room without a window.

As the move-in day grew closer, a door and a closet weren't enough for Max. He wanted a room with a view, and he wanted a full-sized bed too. He hinted at it constantly, saying that he couldn't live in a room without any light or sleep scrunched up in a daybed he'd outgrown.

On our final trim-painting day, Max handed Dad a legit-looking "I PROMISE" contract typed in all caps and everything. Mom was smirking. It was clear she'd helped Max type it up. The gist of Max's contract was that Mom and Dad had to commit to putting a window and bed in his room before he'd set foot in it. At the bottom of the page were four lines for signatures for Max, Mom, Dad, and me. I was the witness.

"What's this?" Dad asked with a chuckle.

This was serious business for Max, and he didn't crack a smile.

Long story short, Dad ended up signing the contract. We all did.

By early August, we had fixed all the major structural things so the house wouldn't cave in on us in our sleep. Inside, the house was still a work in progress, but outside, it was no longer the eyesore on the block. Soft yellow paint had replaced the peeling, drab gray. The door and steps looked nearly normal. A welcoming porch rimmed the front with two jumbo Adirondack chairs on it and a rock-solid railing. Plus, not one boarded-up window.

Moving day was a long one. We got up before the sun came up and loaded our decrepit SUV with boxes of pots and pans, towels and sheets, dishes and glasses, and about a zillion of our other belongings. We crammed our furniture into a mini U-Haul with the help of Dad's gym buddies. Then we lugged it all over to the new place. We did it again and again and again. It took forever.

We were all moved in by lunchtime, exhausted and sweating. I wanted to take a break, but my parents insisted that we start unpacking. "These boxes aren't going to unpack themselves!" Dad said.

Suddenly, there was a knock on the front door. Dad answered it, and we all drifted toward the door in our flip-flops and cut-offs. I was holding two heavy pots.

A woman was standing there in a white midi dress and black patent high heels. Her jet-black bob was sprayed stiff. She looked like she'd just stepped out of an old black-and-white movie. She was a prim and proper relic. Really.

She peered over Dad's shoulder, giving our half-painted living room walls and stacks of boxes a judgy sort of once-over. Then an unexpected smile broke out on her face and she said, "Welcome to the neighborhood. I'm Lily Morris. I live next door."

"Dot, Kat, and Max," Dad said, pointing to each of us.

Mom shook her hand. I nodded. Max slipped under Mom's arm and puffed out his little chest with the big Superman logo on it.

"Oh," Mrs. Morris said to Max. "We might need a superhero's help." She nodded at Mom and Dad. "We've had a string of robberies in our Crystal Park community."

"Oh gosh," Mom said.

"Yep." A frown pinched her brow. "Last week, the thief hit my place and made off with my iPhone, iPad, and laptop in one fell swoop."

"Jeez," Dad said.

Just then, a boy about my age wearing a baseball uniform came running out of the house next door. "Come meet your new neighbors," Mrs. Morris called out, waving him over.

The instant I saw him, my breath caught. He jogged up onto our porch and my eyes went owly wide.

"This is my son, Will," Mrs. Morris said.

Dad repeated our introductions and made some comments about the neighborhood. I wasn't sure what he said because all the small talk faded to white noise. Will was amazing. Drop-your-jaw-straight-to-the-ground fabulous. His deep brown eyes, sprinkled with golden flecks, captured my attention and wouldn't let go.

My head went swimmy with this. Off in the

distance, I vaguely heard Mrs. Morris saying something.

That was when Dad gave me an obvious nudge to bring me out of my reverie.

Max waggled his eyebrows. *Embarrassing.*

I refocused.

Mrs. Morris was looking right at me. "I think you two go to the same school."

I glanced at Will. Tongue-tied, I stammered, "H-hey."

"Hey, yourself," he said, brushing away some sandy curls of hair that dusted his eyes. "Grant," he said, pointing to his chest where the word was scrawled across his pinstriped baseball uniform. "You go there?" The corners of his mouth curled up into an easy smile and sent a rush through every inch of my body.

"Yeah," I said, my voice all crackly. I started to fumble with the kitchen pots and they clattered to the ground. Will helped me gather them and dump them on the porch chair.

"Thanks for the pots," I said, which sounded really dumb. I felt my face flame crimson and examined my feet. *Awkward.*

"Gotta blast," Will said. "Practice." He waved his baseball mitt in the air. "See ya around."

The sun glinted off the golden flecks in his eyes, and my heart beat against my chest. "See ya," I said. My voice trailed off as I watched him run down the street until he turned the corner.

"Well, I'll be going too," said Mrs. Morris, turning on her heels.

After that, I had to sit down and rethink my whole life situation. The house rehab projects would be endless. But if Will was my new neighbor, maybe this house wasn't such a bad idea. A little smile played around my mouth. *Silver linings.*

Chapter 5

Albuquerque loved its ghosts. Tours walked the city streets to hunt them down and tell their stories all year long. My favorite spirit was the six-year-old kid who'd died at the KiMo Theatre and haunted it, playing tricks on the actors if they didn't humor him with donuts. They had proof of it. The donuts put out at night were gone in the morning, and one left behind had little bite marks on it.

Of course, Halloween celebrated all the ghostly spirits and more. No surprise, Grant Middle School got in on it.

"Let your imaginations soar," sputtered Principal Gray's voice over the PA system during morning announcements. "A Halloween dance is scheduled for Friday night on October twenty-ninth. Costumes are required and prizes will be awarded." He cleared his raspy throat and raised his voice. "First prize is a brand-new iPhone." He paused, allowing for student reaction time.

"Second prize: two tickets to the multiplex movie theater. Third prize: sundaes at Ben and Jerry's." He finished by promoting the cost of admission: a can of food.

A food drive was Principal Gray's answer to the hunger problem in Albuquerque, and he wasn't alone. Our first issue of the *Grantline* had endorsed the Student Council's Good Guys Give a Can campaign, which set up drop boxes in homerooms. Our second issue would print the names of those who'd donated because who wouldn't want to see their name in print?

We were only two months into seventh grade, and I was keeping a low profile. I avoided Maria every chance I got and put my sole focus on the *Grantline* and preparing for our big dance.

The entire school was buzzing about the dance. The hallways were filled with conversations about which costumes the students were going to wear. Everyone wanted to be a winner, including me. My old hand-me-down iPhone just wasn't up to snuff, so I desperately needed to win. Besides, I was dying for a way to catch Will's eye. Unpacking and renovating had eaten up a whole month of Sundays and more. In all those weeks, I hadn't said much more than "hey" to Will. I had three weeks to get my costume ready. It was time for me to get on with my life!

Job number 1: Make sure everyone, especially Will, knew about the dance with a front-page story and byline (mine) in the *Grantline*. Principal Gray had rattled off some of the info on morning announcements. It was up to me to flesh out the rest of the details and promote the heck out of Grant Middle School's biggest fall event. I was on it before anyone else could grab the lead story out from under me. I headed straight to the principal's office and signed up for an after-school interview. *Check.*

Job number 2: Piece together a costume that slapped, one that would take first prize and blow Will away. I already had plans to be an e-girl and plenty of time to pull it off. *Check.*

Job number 3: Stop any PTA interference with a high-key editorial on the right to freedom of costume choice. *Check.*

After the last bell rang, I sprinted to my weekly *Grantline* meeting ahead of the rest of the lot. "I've got an interview with the principal at four o'clock," I sang out.

Ms. Ramirez, the paper's sponsor and my favorite teacher, smiled. She had been my sixth-grade English teacher. She made writing fun, particularly on Fridays when we had to write a story-of-the-week paragraph about something inspiring or amusing that happened at school. I loved doing it. She ran the *Grantline*, so I signed up and became the paper's most enthusiastic contributor.

Ms. Ramirez glanced down at her watch. "Better get moving."

And off I went, a reporter with a laser-sharp focus on her job.

I got to the main office a few minutes early with my questions in hand and a big grin on my face. I stood tall, ready to work.

Principal Gray's secretary glanced up. "Change in plans."

My grin shriveled.

She handed me some typed papers. "This should cover it," she said flatly.

Naturally, I pushed her on it. "What if I need a direct quote from the principal?" I smiled at her, trying to soften her up, but it was like talking to an empty desk.

"I think you'll find it in the notes," she said

firmly. She put her head down and went back to work.

My first job had fizzled. Sure, I had notes with key information for school officials. But any real school journalist would want more—at least a face-to-face Q and A about stuff that was not on a fact sheet, like costumes.

On the way out, I peeked into the conference room next to the office. Principal Gray was thick in a convo with the PTA ladies. Last year, some of them had nosed around and created a list of *unsuitable* costumes: the French Maid, the Bad Habit Nun, a bunny. Even Wonder Woman was on their list. E-girl was not.

I hightailed it back to the newspaper room and checked my notes. The PTA had added even more to the list of unsuitable costumes. Some were labeled "too risqué" (the French Maid), while some were "too scary" (Bonnie from *Five Nights at Freddy's*). But disgusting zombies with dripping blood, sunken eyes, and rags for clothes were fine. *Seriously. What are they thinking?* The whole long list ran at the end of the page-one Halloween dance story. My editorial on page two of our four-page newsletter clapped back at the PTA's rules.

Where Do You Draw the Line?

Freedom to choose your own costume might not be an inalienable right under the Constitution, but maybe it should be. Tamping down on the creative inspiration of every Grant Middle School student by putting out a Do Not Wear list is unfair.

Why is a zombie less gross than an alien? Why is a bunny less cute than a dog? It's mostly a matter of taste. Sure, some costumes are inappropriate. A feather with nothing else would be too revealing. Weapons are off-limits. We all agree on that. But Wonder Woman, a nun, or a bunny are mostly fine.

Plus, it's all supposed to be for fun. So, let's not take all the fun out of it by limiting the bazillions of possible costume choices.

My piece was short, to the point, and all about middle-schoolers' student rights. Who could possibly object to that? Not Ms. Ramirez. She had approved my news story and my editorial.

But later that night, my mom read it and said in a warning tone, "I don't know. The PTA ladies might not like it."

Hello? All I did was stand up for a student's right to get a little creative with their Halloween costumes after the PTA rolled out its ridiculously long list of unsuitables.

My mom would have probably been happier if I never questioned any authority—the PTA's or hers. But my job as the editor of the *Grantline* was to get the students' way of thinking on the record, whether it was appreciated by all or not. Besides, it was too late to change anything.

Like I told my mom, "The paper's already gone to press."

Chapter 6

B eyond the wicked perk of my neighbor Will, moving into the house looked like it might be a good idea timing-wise because our family was about to become a plus-one. No, Mom wasn't having another kid. *Thank God.* But Gran was coming to stay with us until, as Mom put it, "we get things sorted out for her."

My grandma had jump-started her life in Florida after my grandpa died. At sixty-five, she joined a group known as the Dancing Dolls, and they entertained retired people around the state. She loved every minute of what she called her "shake-rattle-and-roll for the Boomers."

But a few days ago, Mom got a phone call from one of the Dolls warning that Gran might be in trouble. A fire had broken out in her condo, and she had been rushed to the hospital because she inhaled the fumes. The worst part was that Gran was clueless about how all the smoke had gotten there.

Mom took the first flight to Florida, where the doctors told her that Gran was suffering from memory loss. After that, Mom didn't waste any time clearing out Gran's condo and moving her back to Albuquerque to live with us.

Meanwhile at home, Dad launched our next house project: transform the unlivable guest room—the one with the ginormous crack in the wall—into a safe haven for Gran. None of us wanted to stick so much as a toenail in that room until the new drywall went in. Even then, Max gave that wall a good stiff kick to check if it would hold before we started our work.

Finally, Dad said, "Kat, you're in charge of dusting, vacuuming, and window washing."

I hated that Gran was sick, so I was happy to get the room set up for her. It was a big thumbs-up from me.

He turned to Max. "You're my assistant plasterer for every crack in the wall."

Max nodded and we all got to work.

Later, Dad scrubbed the floors too. At the end of the day, the place didn't look prize-winning, but it was a cut above for sure.

The next day, we all chipped in with the painting. We each took a wall, a roller, and a tub of soft yellow paint. Max wanted to help, but he was making a mess of things, so I helped him finish the small area he had been painting, and Dad painted the fourth wall. When we finished, the room looked as bright as sunshine.

A day later, we moved a twin bed from my room. We dressed it up with crisp white bed-clothes and placed a stack of fresh towels on top. Then we added a night table, lamp, and a dresser from my parents' room. To finish it off, we hung up family photos on three walls to wrap around the bed and give Gran a homey feel.

"Magnifico!" Dad said with a swish of his hand across the newly polished space.

"Wait," I said. "It needs something more." I ran outside and picked some fresh black-eyed Susans that Mom had planted in the yard. I placed them in a vase on the table next to the music box with a tiny dancer on top that Gran had given me a long time ago.

We all grinned. *Perfection*.

———

Gran's first full day at home was a sunny Saturday. We had all just returned from the gym, wired and set to get on with what was left of our day.

Dad announced that he was going to fire up the grill, and Gran said she had an appetite to whip up one of her fancy cherry pies. She was old but still full of life. She didn't even have any gray hair.

Mom elected me to run down the street to the grocery store with Gran. Max whined that he wanted to come too, so off we went.

At the store, we collected flour, milk, eggs, sugar, gelatin, and two pounds of fresh cherries. We were next in line and placed our items on the counter when a big muscly guy squeezed in ahead of us.

He plunked down his grape gum in front of our cherries. "Can I push in here? I just have this one item," he said.

Gran pulled her head all the way back into her neck. "No, you can wait your turn like everyone else." She pushed the packet of gum away from our food.

"Gran, let it go," I said, hoping to shelf any noisy face-off over almost nothing.

But Gran wasn't having it. She stood up straighter and glared at Gum Guy. The woman behind us made a tongue-clucking *tsk* sound. The man behind her flicked his fingers back and forth, motioning for all of us to move on.

Gum Guy moved his gum back and said, "Hey, old lady, I'm in a hurry."

Max grabbed the gum from the counter and stared at the guy. "You can't talk to Gran like that."

The big guy snatched the gum from Max's hand.

Max puffed out his Superman chest. I guess he was counting on his superpowers to kick in so he could stand up to the Hulk.

Meanwhile, a group of bystanders had formed behind us, and Gum Guy backed off. The jerk-face scrambled out of there and cheers erupted. One man even gave Gran and Max an ear-splitting whistle.

Gran and Max beamed.

I scanned the crowd to see if anyone I knew had witnessed the flare-up. I half expected Maria to be waiting in line to snap a picture of the crazy, old lady and nutso kid—and me.

The walk home was quiet . . . for me. Max talked excitedly about what had happened at the store, and Gran kept saying he was a hero.

I tried to tune them out. Everything had happened so fast in the store. I didn't know why, but I'd frozen up. I should have been the one to stand up to that guy, not Max or Gran. But who was I kidding? I couldn't even stand up to Maria.

Back at the house, Gran spread out all her carefully collected ingredients on the kitchen counter and stared at them, puzzled.

"I don't think I feel much like cherry pie anymore," she said.

"Come on," Mom said. "We can pull up a perfectly good recipe online."

"If that's what you want to do, you make the pie," Gran grumbled. Then she headed out of the room in a hurry.

Worry lines crisscrossed Mom's face. She whispered something to Dad, then they went after Gran. They were in her room for a long time, fussing over stuff in muffled voices that I couldn't make out. Afterward, I needled them about their chat, but they were all don't-breathe-a-word about it. Even so, I knew such a spun-out talk must've been about more than pie.

Sometimes I felt like I would burst with frustration over how my parents still treated me like a little kid. I was twelve—almost thirteen—old enough to buy the groceries and babysit Max, and old enough to know what was going on.

Later, Mom sent Dad to the store for whipped

cream. She served it over the fresh cherries for dessert.

"Delicious," said Gran, smiling, without a single mention of baking her pie.

Chapter 7

Sunday meant home improvement duty for everyone. *Ugh*. Would it ever end? Fixing up Gran's room had been kind of fun. But being stuck in the house every Sunday afternoon was not. Even Gran wasn't off the hook. And no excuses worked either.

Our gym had always closed a half-day early on Sundays. It used to be for family time, whether we liked it or not. No friends, no phones, no video games—just the fam. *Bad enough*. We used to go out to a movie, a museum, the zoo, or a restaurant. Of course, the downswing at the gym swallowed up most of our fun money. Since we moved, the house sucked up the rest of it, and Sunday afternoons were for project time only.

Today we were painting Max's room. Dad had patched up a bunch of hairline cracks and filled in a hole that would be big enough to see through once the window was installed. He moved on to the long, drawn-out chore of stripping away the ugly rose wallpaper in my room with some special solution, and a scraper and putty knife to shave away all the stubborn leftovers. Mom and Gran were in the kitchen lining the cabinet shelves with paper as they slugged down veggie smoothies.

Max and I were set up in his room with rollers and paint pans. We'd been given the okay to pick the paint color for our rooms. *Bad idea*. Max picked a gross green.

"It looks like puke," I said, clutching my stomach like I was about to hurl.

"It's army green," Max said, pouting. "The color of warriors."

"Funny," I said. "Get rolling. Long strokes."

Dip . . . stroke . . . up . . . down.

Dip . . . stroke . . . up . . . down.

And so it went for about an hour until Dad came to check on us.

"Hey, Dad," I said over my shoulder. "Aren't there child labor laws about this kind of thing?"

Dad chuckled. "Nope."

"I may have to check with Child Services on that. I'm just saying."

He told me I was doing a terrific job and to get back to it.

Then he jumped in to help Max. "Let's put some more paint on the roller, son. And push it up and down, not sideways. Like so . . ."

Max had a go at it.

Dad demoed again.

Max gave it another shot.

Dad demoed once more.

Max gave it his all, and he actually was getting a little better at it.

———————

Meanwhile, my editorial had gone viral around school. No surprise that the week after the paper came out, I got a lot of high fives and slaps on the back everywhere I went. Playful arm punches and fist pumps ruled my day.

I bounced into my *Grantline* club meeting, floating on air. I could barely feel my feet touch the ground. That was how good I felt, and I couldn't wait to ramp up my message with another top-line editorial.

As usual, I was the first one in the room, and Ms. Ramirez—the best club sponsor ever—greeted me with a solid, "What's up?"

"The feedback's been amazing," I raved.

"Good," she said. But her voice was flat, and there was only a piddly little smile on her face.

My high deflated. "Something wrong?"

"Principal Gray . . . it seems he got a mouthful of pushback from the PTA ladies. I'm afraid they're demanding a change of tone in the *Grantline's* editorials."

I couldn't help from screwing up my face. "Do we have to listen to *them*?"

"We have to listen to Principal Gray."

My mouth dropped.

Ms. Ramirez usually stuck up for the students. She promoted student voices. It was what I liked most about her. I couldn't wrap my head around her backing Principal Gray and the PTA. It flew in the face of everything our paper stood for, especially the editorial page.

"What about freedom of the press?" I asked her. "What about student rights?" My questions just hung in the air.

By this time, other club members were dribbling into the room, and we caught them up. Mostly, they took my side against the PTA, but there wasn't enough support to do anything about it.

"The topic's too narrow . . . Halloween costumes," said DJ, quarterback of the football team and our sports writer. "How about an editorial pushing for half-day Fridays for athletics?"

"Yeah, right," said Billy Taswell, arts enthusiast on the entertainment beat. "Like everyone can get behind that."

"Pizza parties for honor roll students," suggested Ruby Sanchez, straight-A honor roll student and our go-to news writer.

I gave them all a long look. "The message is a student's right to choose," I pointed out. "Not perks for jocks or brainiacs."

We went around and around about this without a whole lot of consensus. Finally, we tabled the topic and got down to our regular business of handing out stories for the next issue and posting them on the *Grantline* assignment board. Before we left, Ms. Ramirez wrote "TBA" in the editorial slot, and my mouth twisted into a frown.

"Need to cool it for now," Ms. Ramirez said to me on the way out. Then she threw me a wink and a nod. "Doesn't mean we'll never publish another hot-button editorial."

I smiled. I could already feel another editorial bubbling up inside of me.

Chapter 8

I'd pieced together my costume. No small job. First off, I bought pink hair dye, an absolute must-have for my e-girl look. Then I pulled together my outfit—a black-and-white-striped crop top and a pink graphic tee to throw over it, a black pleated miniskirt, and some black fishnet tights—all scrounged from my closet and a local thrift shop. I swung by the party store for a mixed bag of tattoos—hearts and butterflies, skulls and bones—and a full makeup kit with heavy black eyeliner for winged eyes, and blazing pink blush and lipstick for the big round lip and bright-cheek look. E-girl was good to go.

Tough luck, but just as I was set to prep on the night of the dance, Mom popped by my room unexpectedly. I thought my whole aesthetic was on point. Mom did not.

She lowered her glasses—never a good sign—and caught sight of the bottle of hair dye. "No way are you dyeing your hair pink." Then she spotted my tattoos. "Those skulls and bones are creepy. If your teacher sees those things, she'll send you home."

"My teacher's woke."

Mom jerked her head back. "I do not appreciate your tone." She planted her hands on her hips like she meant business. "Your teacher may be *woke,* but she is not going to see that costume," she said firmly.

I cut back on my tone a sliver. "It's just a costume," I coaxed.

She pinched her face, unconvinced.

I pressed on. "In case you hadn't noticed, I'm an e-girl."

Mom did that squeezing-her-eyes-shut business.

Fashion was not my parents' thing. E-girl was certainly beyond their orbit of style. They wore boring gym clothes most of the time. Mom pulled her hair up into a no-frills ponytail, and Dad went completely hairless and shaved his whole head.

Still, on the edge of forty, they were amazingly fit. Dad had muscles and tight abs from all his weight training. Mom was slim—a total pretzel—from the yoga she taught. Lately, she'd added mindful meditation exercises to her classes, to cut down on stress, she said. I wished she would channel some of those exercises now.

"I . . . DON'T . . . HAVE . . . ANY . . . OTHER . . . COSTUME!" I cried in a last push to save e-girl from extinction.

Mom's voice rose even higher in pitch than mine. "But I do!" she said, ridiculously excited.

She turned on her heels without another word and left the room. She returned in a flash with a hideous childish costume that she bounced up and down in front of me.

My eyes bulged. Green and yellow mismatched stockings, a yellow shapeless smock over a baggy green shirt, and a red wig with braided pigtails that stuck out sideways like a bug's antenna.

"What is that Pippi Longstocking costume doing here?" I asked, horrified.

"I bought it for you," she said with a broad smile.

I wrinkled my nose at her. "Mooooooom," I whined. "I can't."

"And I can't think of why you wouldn't want to dress as a true feminist with a generous heart."

"She's nine," I said.

Mom gave me her big-eyed *so what* look.

Pippi Longstocking had been my favorite storybook heroine when I was a kid. She was strong, independent, and did not tolerate bullies. Sometimes she made fun of snooty adults who looked down on her. She was great, but she was a child. I was almost thirteen, and my mom did not seem to accept that.

I tried to flat-out refuse the idea of wearing the ridiculous getup. "I can't!" I yelled. "I'd rather show up as *anything* but Pippi, even Miss Piggy."

But Mom didn't budge.

I really, *really* wanted to go to the dance. I couldn't even believe how much I wanted to go to that dance. In the end, I did. Dad drove me over to school, where I hesitated, sucked in a deep breath, and walked through the door as the one and only Pippi, with sideways pigtails and the silliest mismatched stocking outfit ever.

First thing, I dropped my Campbell's soup can into a huge cobwebbed basket that looked like spooky clawed hands reaching up to grab it. Then I scoped out the costumes. Lots of familiar store-boughts showed up—vampires and werewolves, devils and angels, cats and gorillas,

Maleficent, Barbie and Ken, and a bunch of others.

Among the originals was Jen as Partly Cloudy in a baby-blue leotard with gobs of puffy cotton plastered everywhere, and a big Save the Planet sign that made it hit different.

Maria was dressed as the sun, with a huge yellow cardboard circle hanging in front of her and planets bobbing all around. Luce, Maria's bestie and sidekick bully, was the moon, a smaller and duller circle.

And then there was me—Pippi.

Jen stared at my costume. She laughed and pinched my cheek. "So cute."

I shrugged and curtsied.

Most kids left me alone, probably because they didn't know who I was supposed to be or didn't care. Still, no surprise, I had to put up with some tougher judges, like Maria.

"Who's the little pigtail girl over there?" she asked in her snottiest voice. She sidled up beside me with her sun and planets jiggling. "Well, little Miss Goody Two-Shoes," she said nastily. "I thought we left all of our baby costumes back at the elementary school."

Luce raced over and copycatted her. "Yeah, with our pigtails."

Maria tugged on one of my pigtails. They both broke out into fits of laughter.

I froze. I couldn't think of one smart thing to say back to them, and my feet felt glued to the spot.

Meanwhile, others had drifted over toward the commotion and circled around me. Some of them were joining in with hand-cupped giggles.

So, being surrounded by a bunch of kids with their wide eyes staring at me and their big mouths laughing at me in the middle of a school dance totally sucked.

Then, in a flat second, everything changed. Their mouths shut and their eyes bounced from me to the legendary Captain Jack Sparrow, a.k.a. Will Morris, as he latched onto Maria's sun circle and hauled her away from me.

My heart rate doubled.

"Get off!" Maria yelled, yanking her costume free from the pirate. Luce raced over to help her.

But Will brandished his fake sword and pointed it at Luce's heart as if he were ready to slash it in two. "Don't even think it," he warned. Then Jen dashed over and stood next to him.

I held my breath.

After a stony stare-down, Maria and Luce backed off. "Who wants to hang around someone who still wears pigtails, anyway," said Maria, guarding her sun and planets as she swept off with Luce, the moon, trailing behind her.

With the tormentors gone, the daring pirate and me—the innocent damsel—locked eyes. It was a storybook. But before either of us could say a word, one of the chaperones came rushing over to split us up. Worse, the chaperone jumped to my defense.

"You are just too adorable to be picked on," she said, sheltering me with her arm like I was a small child who needed her protection. *Cringe.* *CRINGE.*

That really got things rolling. The kids around me started in with a bunch of wisecracks while Will slipped away.

"Poor little orphan girl," crooned one kid.

"Tallyho, pigtails," called out another.

After that, I didn't know how the dance went. My humiliation factor was too high. I took off for the girls' bathroom.

"Kat," Jen called, coming after me.

I was past consoling. "Go back to the dance," I

said, shooting out my arm to stop her. "I'm going home."

For a fraction of a second, I thought, *If I could only go back, strike up a chat with Will, or maybe have a dance with him.* But the fiery girl who wrote blistering editorials had gone AWOL. I called my dad and hung out in a bathroom stall until he came.

"How was the dance?" Dad asked on the way home.

I had nothing, nada, zero. I just stared out the car window as the street signs and houses slid by until my eyes brimmed with hot tears, blurring everything. At home, I dashed to my room, ripped off the stupid costume, and buried it in the stupid trash can where it belonged.

———————

Later, when Jen got home from the dance, she called me. I was a mopey mess, so she did most of the talking.

"I danced with Chip!" she cried.

"Congrats," I said, uninspired.

"And you're talking to a second-place contest winner," she said in her sunny way.

I was happy for her. I was. But I was stuck in my mood. So I sighed one of those end-of-the-world sighs and asked in a low-key way, "Who won first?"

"Um . . . well . . ." Finally, she blurted it out. "The Sun."

I groaned.

"Sorry. Will asked about you, though."

You could have knocked me over with a feather. I perked up. "Really?"

"Mm-hmm."

I didn't know why she didn't lead with this sensational—*breathtaking*—detail, but I was floating too high to chew her out about it because it gave me LIFE.

I was dying to hear more. "Word-for-word what did he say?"

"I think he said, 'Where's Kat?'"

I swooned. "He's so cute."

"And a third-place costume winner."

"Yay!" Then, recalling that sparkling moment when the daring pirate swooped in to save me from the evil clutches of Maria, I said, "He's my knight in pirate's clothing."

Chapter 9

After weeks of no real strategy to shake things up—except maybe my failed costume—this was my chance. I was on a mission. And Will was my target. My parents had decided a few days ago to invite the neighborhood crew over for a get-together. They opted for a short-prep, low-budget Halloween yard party on Sunday afternoon with cider and treats.

Mom bought loads of candy corn. She had twenty-five packages of assorted flavors of the stuff. Who knew candy corn came in root beer flavor? And she baked about a hundred designer-level cupcakes, all orange and covered with gobs of swirly icing. They had pictures on toothpicks of all kinds of fall symbols, like pumpkins, leaves, witches, and ghosts.

"Hey, it's just a block party, not a city-wide fall festival," Dad said.

"You can never be too prepared," Mom shot back.

Dad's big contribution to the party was the game center in the backyard. It had an apple-bobbing station for the younger kids and a card table for takers of any age. But the real showpiece of the gaming area was the miniature golf course that Dad had worked on a little at a time since mid-week. It was a four-hole course, and it didn't feature any fancy loop-the-loops or windmills, but it did have obstacles. The first hole was a straight shot, but the second had blocks of wood jutting out. The third had a tunnel, and the last hole had a pretty steep incline for an uphill battle to the finish.

The party was at two o'clock. At about one, Dad put the finishing touches on his golf course. Mom and Gran set fifty of the cupcakes next to the cider and piles of candy corn on the folding table with the orange-and-black paper tablecloth. Jen and I added decorative cups, plates, and napkins. Then we helped Dad set up a bunch of folding chairs in groups for chatting. Everything appeared ready.

Gran lowered herself into a lawn chair not far from the food table. Max and our bulldog, Moe, came to keep Gran company. Mom, Dad, Jen, and I headed off to change into our party clothes.

Naturally, I had to look awesome. I wore vintage wide-legged jeans and paired them with a white T-shirt with all the planets of the universe splashed over the front in flashy neon pink. Down the back, the cursive lettering, also in pink neon, said: *My Exciting Mind Could Send Unusual Notions Pondering Eternally.* I liked a tee with a message.

About half an hour later when Jen and I walked back outside, we stopped dead in our tracks. Max, Moe, and Gran had given the treats a dry-run sampling before showtime. They'd gone through about a quarter of the cupcakes.

"Mom!" I yelled. "You'd better get out here!"

Mom came running. Her mouth formed a big *O*. Max's hands and Moe's paws were covered with orange goo. Half of one cupcake dribbled out of Moe's mouth, and Max's shirt was pasted with the sticky gunk. Moe drooled. Max smacked his lips and giggled.

I pointed to Gran. "Look."

"What?" asked Mom.

"Look closer," Jen said.

Then Gran stood up to see what all the fuss was about, and Mom noticed that Gran's dress pockets were bulging.

"What have you got there?" Mom asked her.

"Nothing," said Gran. "Just saving a cup-cake."

But her memory was playing tricks on her again. She'd actually tucked away another cupcake, and another, until her pockets were stuffed with them. Suddenly aware of what she'd done, she tried to hide them by smashing them flat with her arms, but the icing oozed out of her pockets and coated the front of her dress.

Sure, I felt terrible for Gran, but I couldn't help throwing up my hands. "You know what? The whole neighborhood's going to think we're a bunch of cupcake crazies."

Mom gave me one of her *don't-start* looks, so I shut up. But she knew what I meant. A big reason we were even throwing this party was to create goodwill among the neighbors in hopes of boosting gym membership.

Party time was only thirty minutes away. Mom flew into action. "Sam!" she screamed. When Dad came rushing out, she whisked Max over to him. "Clean him up right now. And toss Moe into the shed." She pointed at Jen and me. "Get some trash bags and clean up all the leftover cake chunks and wrappers." She turned to Gran. "You come with me. Let's get you a clean dress without pockets."

When Mom reappeared with Gran, she told me to keep an eye on her. She backtracked to the kitchen and whipped up more cupcakes. By the time the guests arrived, we were all in our proper places, ready to meet and greet our unsuspecting visitors. It was a regular family triumph.

Jen and I were standing in the corner of the yard, people-watching. We'd spent hours talking tactics for ensnaring the love of my life while we were setting up for the party. Every time someone new came into the yard, my heart sped up a bit, hoping it was Will.

"What if I walk over to Will as soon as he comes in and say, 'Thanks for the dance assist'?"

Jen tilted her head. "Maybe ease into the convo before you hammer him with that."

"Like how?" I needed something smart and catchy.

"Well, you're the hostess. It's expected you offer to serve him whatever his lil ol' heart desires. How about, 'At your service: cider, cup-cake, or *me*'?" she said with a naughty little smile.

We both dissolved into a fit of giggles, shushing ourselves, but loudly. Nearby, Max heard us and started giggling too. I didn't want the human sponge hanging around, soaking stuff up and spewing it out to the universe.

"Hey," I said. "Get lost, Nosey."

"No," he said with a solid shake of his thick dark mop of hair. Then he crossed his arms and spread his feet like he wasn't going anywhere.

I was forced to resort to sending him on a wild goose chase to find an imaginary man passing out free Superman T-shirts in front of our house.

Unfortunately, Mom hurried him right back to the yard and told me to stop playing my silly tricks on him. Max blew a cranberry at me and went off chanting, "Kattie likes Will, Kattie likes Will . . ."

If Jen hadn't been there, I probably would have gone after him, pinned him down, and made him promise to never breathe a word about anything he'd heard if he valued his life. As things were, I let it go. I slathered on an extra layer of pink lip gloss, poured some cider into a cup, picked up a cupcake, and practiced in my head what I was going to say.

Just then, Will walked in from the side gate, looking totally clean-cut and classy in his army-green cargos and fitted ribbed polo.

And I froze. All of my carefully thought-out phrases flew out the window. All I could think was, *Uhhh . . .*

Jen pushed me forward. I stumbled clumsily into him before painfully squeezing out one full word. "Cupcake?"

Will smiled awkwardly. He reached out and took the cupcake and cider from my hands. Then he was gone.

I turned to Jen. "I feel like such an idiot. How bad was that?"

She shrugged. "Not *that* bad . . ."

"Oh my God. I think I'm going to die of embarrassment. It was awful, and—"

"Stop being so extra. It's not that big of a deal."

I gave her big eyes.

"Look, even if it was terrible, it's your party and there's no place else to go."

Well, that's a gross lack of cuddly support from my alleged bestie.

"Your empathy runneth over," I said and

sagged down on one of the folding chairs. Jen sank down in a chair beside me, looking almost as glum. Maybe she felt sorry for me. I couldn't really tell because just a minute later, she perked up.

"Look," she said. "Will's hanging out with Chip at the golf course."

Chip's hair was gelled and slicked back. His baggy cut-off jeans hung loose on his hips, showing off his baseball-bat boxers sticking out at the top. He probably thought he was so trendy. Jen obviously thought so too. But I thought he looked like he was trying too hard.

"Come on," Jen said. "Let's play golf."

"I can't." I meant that I didn't know how, but Jen wasn't letting me explain.

"You can." She tugged me by the arm and dragged me into a game with the boys.

"Okay," she said to Will and Chip. "Here's the deal. We challenge you guys to a game of golf. If we win, you have to bob for apples with the babies. If you win, you score some delish cupcakes while we do the apple bobbing."

The guys appeared less than impressed.

"Unless you're afraid to take on the two true champions of this course," she quickly added.

"Right," Chip said, smirking. "We accept your lame challenge with fair warning that we are trained golfers who have won championships on courses way more difficult than this one."

"Yeah right," said Jen. "Then let the games begin."

After some fooling around, picking the right club and ball color, we got started.

"Girls first," called Jen, breezing past the boys. She performed one of those bowing movements and waved me forward with a swish of her arm. "Kat, your course, your shot."

I suppose she had some wacky idea that I'd hit a hole in one since the game was in my yard. *Not happening.* I stepped forward. What choice did I have? With a shaky hand, I took my first stroke at the easiest of the four holes. It turned out to be too dainty a shot. My ball went only halfway to the hole. Heat rushed to my cheeks. I tried to shake it off and sound laid-back.

"Just getting a feel for the course," I said to a bunch of blank stares. I took a deep breath and gladly moved back out of the spotlight.

"Uh-huh," said Will, stepping up for his shot, which turned out to be a hole in one.

"Not bad," I said. "Of course, anyone can have

a lucky first shot. It could have been better." I was determined to play this cool . . . well, semi-cool.

"How?" he laughed. "How could it have been better?"

I shrugged and looked the other way.

Jen was up next.

"Give it some punch," said Chip, swaggering over to position himself to her left.

I guess Jen didn't want to make the same mistake I had made. She took his advice and whacked the ball as hard as she could, but her aim was off. It jumped the course, veered to the left, and socked Chip in the shin.

"Ouch!" he yelled.

"Oops," she said.

I clamped my hand over my mouth to stifle a fit of giggles, and Will cleared his throat to hide a smile.

Chip leveled a squinty-eyed death glare at us as he rubbed the red mark on his leg. "Seriously? We're playing with amateurs," he said in disgust.

Jen raised an eyebrow. "Oh, and you're a pro?"

"I am compared to you." He shot her a really cold look.

She waved him off. "Oh, chill. It was an accident, okay? You'll live."

Chip sucked it up and stepped forward. "I'll show you how it's done," he said in his stuck-uppity way. His ball went past the hole. It took him two tries to finish.

Okay, so Chip was pretty good, and Will had hit a hole in one. Still, the game wasn't over. We could rally. I stretched out my arm to Jen for a fist bump.

On the second hole, I accidentally tapped Will's arm just as he was swinging.

"Interference," he called.

"Stuff happens," I said.

He gave me a side-eye. "I'm gonna whip your butt anyway."

Fine by me. The truth was, I didn't care if he did. I was talking to Will, he was talking to me, and that was all that really mattered. My biggest fantasy was materializing. Of course, it wasn't a perfect fantasy. When I hit my fifth ball hard enough to go up the hill on the last hole, it skidded off the green and into the apple-bobbing bucket. Water splashed up into the face of the surprised bobber. Everyone's attention focused on him, then on the golf ball he pulled out of the bucket, and finally on me, the girl on the golf course whose club remained frozen in midair.

Surprise turned to laughter. First, the bucket crowd shrieked with laughter, and then Chip, Will, and Jen were in stitches. I—the laughingstock—barely smiled. I marked the number five as my final score. No one dared to object.

When everyone settled down, it was clear— the guys had run away with the game. We were having too much fun, though, to go down that easily.

Jen's green eyes twinkled. "Best out of three?" she tried.

They went along with it, and we were heavy into the second round when a loud clap of thunder suspended play. Everyone ran to take cover in our living room, toting the party cider, cupcakes, and all—plus the cheap folding table covered with now-soggy crepe paper.

Will, Chip, Jen, and I headed for the food table. As soon as we got there, Will handed me a cupcake with a witch on top. I was so surprised that I almost dropped it.

Some serious doubt crept up inside. "Why a witch?" I asked as casually as I could.

"You remind me of the Good Witch of the North from the Land of Oz."

I blushed. "Good answer." Then I handed him a cupcake with a ghost on it.

He crinkled his forehead. "Spooky."

"No," I said, smiling. "You're like Casper the Friendly Ghost."

"Ah, from that old movie."

"What ghost?" Max asked, suddenly appearing at my elbow.

"Go away, Max," I said.

"Nuh-uh," he said. Then he started chanting, "Kattie and Will sittin' in a tree, Kattie and Will sittin' in a tree . . ." And as if that weren't enough, he puckered his lips, sucked in a lot of air, and started making disgusting smooching noises. *SMACK. SMAAAACK. SMAAAAAAAACK!*

I turned as red as those bobbing apples. "Shut up, or you're toast," I hissed through gritted teeth.

That was when he took off and ratted me out to Dad, who came at me all shouty and told me in front of everyone, including Will, to "stop terrorizing Max," which was even more humiliating than Max's chanting and fake kissing, if that was even possible. *Ugh.*

The rain had stopped. Without a single dry chair to sit on or even a tray to set a drink on, the party was breaking up. Everyone was filing out of the house. Will probably felt bad for me because he gave me a weak smile and said, "Great party." Then he and Chip left too.

That was how my day ended. *Not perfect.* Thank God the stuff with Will balanced out the stuff with the family and the house.

Scrap that . . . the stuff with Will MORE than balanced it out!

Chapter 10

Our party was over, but another one was in the works. A few of our neighbors decided on the spur of the moment to keep the party rolling with a potluck dinner. Mom, Dad, and Gran were invited, but that meant someone else would have to take Max trick-or-treating. Mom elected—surprise—guess who?

"I'm too old for dressing up and begging people for candy," I said. I did not mention the obvious, that Max had embarrassed the daylights out of me earlier that day.

Mom must have had some notion that there was bad blood between Max and me, but she didn't let on. Instead, she got all twisty with my words, saying that I might be too old but Max was not, and it would be mean not to take him. She punched out the word *mean* much louder than the rest so that it resounded throughout the room.

"I don't think it's too much to ask," she said. "Do you?"

Mom, Dad, Gran, Jen, Max—all five pairs of their judgmental eyes fastened on me.

Did I have a choice? No, I did not have a choice. None.

I sucked in my cheeks. "Okay," I said.

A little later, Mom, Dad, and Gran packed up some of the leftover cupcakes and set out for their dinner party, and Jen and I got down to business in my bedroom.

"If we're gonna do the door-to-door thing," Jen said, "I think we should go extra, costumes and all."

"Not happening." I had nixed the costume thing after the Pippi thing. I'd never be caught dead in a Halloween costume ever again. No way. And that was final.

"Kat," Jen said as if she was telepathic. "A *grown-up* costume will be the perfect way to grab Will's attention."

I hesitated. "I don't know."

She kept egging me on. "Your parents won't be home to see your costume this time."

True. Mom couldn't mind if she didn't find out. Of course, she'd freak out if she did find out, and I'd never hear the end of it. But what if I could resurrect e-girl and wow Will as I'd originally planned?

I grinned. "Fine. We'll be e-girls . . . and e-boy." First, I held up a bottle. "We'll dye our hair pink." Then I showed off my oh-so-carefully-assembled-but-never-worn e-girl costume.

"Hot," Jen said.

She didn't have all of my gear. What she did have was a hugely oversized T-shirt with an enormous Billie Eilish graphic that she'd brought for our sleepover. Her super baggy jeans made it the absolutely perfect grungy e-girl outfit.

"Let's use tattoos," I said. I pulled out a bag of mixed paste-on strips from my dresser drawer and dangled them. I grabbed the hearts. Jen snatched up the butterflies.

Max got the skull-and-bone leftovers. We stamped them all over his face and arms to fancy up his black jeans and tee. Then Jen rifled through a box of my hair stuff and pulled out a tube of gel. We sprayed his hair pink, then Jen spiked his whole head with gel, adding a shockingly cool edge to his goth-ness.

"Pink?" asked Max, studying his hair. He tapped at the tips. He shrugged it off and pointed to the tattoos on his arms. "Excellent." He wiggled his fingers up and down, ghostlike. "*Scaaaaary,*" he said.

Last thing, Jen and I glowed up with my face paint for the thick-winged eye and extra-heavy blush look. Max got a small black mask to wear over his face in place of our vampy makeup.

And off we went.

The first stop on our trick-or-treat trail was at the Barlows, our next-door neighbors and the sweetest old retired couple you'd ever meet, who always gave a big *hello* to everyone. They were outside their front door to welcome us before we could even get to their porch.

"Look at you. You're all very pretty in your pink hairdos," said Mrs. Barlow. "Cheeks just like roses," she said, smiling at me. *Major kudos for my signature e-girl blush.* She patted the tips of Max's pointy hair and laughed.

"Those are some frightening tattoos," Mr. Barlow said. "We'd better turn over some of our booty." He scrunched his face and dropped a candy bar into each of our bags.

Max lifted his mask. "Don't be scared, Mr. Barlow. It's just us."

Mr. Barlow relaxed. "Oh. You scared the

bejesus out of me," he said, which sent Max into fits of laughter.

It was fun like that all the way around the neighborhood, and I was even beginning to think Jen had been right about the costumes. Then, just as we were finishing up our rounds, a scruffy-looking guy wearing a ski mask and carrying a bulging black trash bag thrown over his shoulder emerged from between two houses. He streaked across the lawn and pulled up short right next to us on the sidewalk. His big bag bounced off his shoulder and pounded to the ground with a thud.

I nearly jumped out of my skin. Jen edged herself backward. Max stood his ground like a wannabe superhero.

"Is that a costume?" Max asked, reaching up to touch the guy's ski mask.

I snatched his hand. "No, Max," I said.

"Dang kids," snarled the man. He glared at us for a second through his creepy cutout eyeholes. Then he slung his bag over his shoulder and took off in the other direction.

Max hollered after the guy as he rounded the corner. "Scaredy-cat. What's in the bag, kids' candy?"

No answer from the guy. *Thank God.*

The incident put a damper on our e-kid vibe, but we still had to visit Will's house no matter what. We hadn't run into him trick-or-treating, and his house was dark. We knocked and rang the bell. No answer. We circled the house and peeped in the windows. Nothing. There we were, all dressed to impress, and nada.

Bummer.

When we walked into my house, I was still debating whether I should hang out in my costume a little longer in case Will came home. I checked to see if the lights were on at his place, like every other minute. I was pretty deep in thought about it and didn't even look up until I heard my mom's voice cut through the air.

"Oh no."

The sharp edge of it stopped me cold. *Uh-oh. Busted.* A face-off with my mom had never been part of the plan. I'd gambled on my parents being out late and the whole punk vibe gone by the time they rolled through the door.

"What are you even doing home so early?" I asked.

"More cupcakes for the party," Dad said as he held up a box of them.

Mom just squinted her eyes at us. "What kind of costumes are those?"

"Modern, twenty-first-century ones," I said.

Mom's tight lips matched her slit eyes, and she went on and on about how she couldn't believe we went parading around the neighborhood dressed like that, and how people must've thought we were some crazy street kids or the Crystal Park burglars, and—

"Maybe," I said. I didn't think it was the right time to tell her about our run-in with the possible *real* burglar.

Mom steamed for a bit. Then she whipped off her glasses and whirled them around in circles at Max's head. "Kat Cruz, I never thought you'd do *this* to your little brother."

"I like my hair," Max squealed. "I wanna keep it for school."

I ran my fingers over the tips of his hair. "See, he likes it. Chill."

Our convo hit a full stop as Mom stewed over my words. Then she said to Max in a firm but sugary way, "Sweetie, time to take off the pink points and tattoos." She fired me her death glare, and all the sugar spilled out of her. "I don't like any of it," she said, her voice slow, clear, and loud.

I got it. She didn't like e-girls. But I couldn't be her Pippi forever.

"It's all for fun," I said to calm her down.

Jen stood by me. "Right, for fun."

Mom just did that squeezing-her-eyes-shut business.

I tossed her a light smile. "The stuff washes right off or will eventually wear off."

I didn't mean to set her off again, but my little joke drove her around the bend. "Don't get smart with me," she said. "Get some shampoo, soap, and water and show me." She crossed her arms and parked herself there, her face full of frown lines.

At last, Dad intervened with some happy talk about the holiday spirit and the out-and-out fun of Halloween. But mostly he gave us a lecture about not blowing up this "costume spat" into something more than it was.

It took a minute to sink in, but Mom finally uncrossed her arms. The tight lines radiating from her eyes and lips softened.

I took a deep breath and said, "Max, pink is

only special for Halloween. We'll do it again next year."

"With skulls and bones? Promise?"

I threw a quick glance over my shoulder at my mother. "I promise."

Chapter 11

G ran spent her mornings at Cruz's Athletic Club. She took an aerobics class and then hung out afterward to read the *Albuquerque Journal* and occasionally the *Grantline*. Sometimes she helped take inventory of the equipment or check in members at the desk. Around noon, Mom drove her home for lunch and left her there alone until I got back from school. It seemed to be working out, minus a couple of mishaps.

Once, Gran had left the water running in the hall bathroom with the sink stopper down. Water flooded the hall and part of the living room while she snoozed on the sofa. It caused a major mop-up job, but it wasn't the end of the world. Another time, Moe got locked out of the house, probably when Gran went to get the mail. We found Moe a block over, tearing up a neighbor's vegetable patch. Dad replaced the chomped veggies and replanted the trampled plants. Again, nothing to get that excited about.

This was different. Today when I got home, the place was empty, with no Gran planted in front of the TV, napping in her room, or anywhere. I called Mom and Dad right away, and they raced over to the house. We all jumped into our ramshackle SUV and searched the neighborhood. We clanked up beside her several blocks away.

"Where are you headed?" Dad asked.

Gran screwed up her face. "Just takin' a walk," she mumbled.

Mom wrinkled her forehead and asked her if she knew her way home.

Gran took a long look around. She refocused her expressionless stare back on us.

Dad winked at her. "Why don't you hop in the car with us?"

She squinted her eyes. She took a step forward, then hesitated and stayed put. Max leaped out of the car, scrambled over to her, and latched onto her arm. She glanced down at him. A trace of a smile broke out on her face, and she let him guide her to the car. I helped her climb into the back seat and looped my arm around her shoulder. Her head sank down against my chest. She was quiet the whole way home. It felt so weird because she was not acting like the Gran I knew at all.

The next day, Mom started her hunt for an assisted-living home where Gran could get more looking after for her Alzheimer's. Mom began with a rah-rah attitude. Gran had more of a couldn't-care-less mindset. No big surprise. She had barely adjusted to her move back to Albuquerque to live with us. Now she was being shuttled to a special-care place for old people with memory troubles where she wouldn't know anyone. I really wished Mom would just let Gran stay put.

Mom made calls anyway and drew up a list of must-haves, with security at the top. She was ready for on-site visits and scouting for helpers. Dad said he had a million things to do at the gym and couldn't help. Gran sniffled, pretending she was too sick to help. The last choice, Mom turned her eyes on me. "Kat, I need feedback. For Gran?"

I became her helpmate.

We checked out the cheapest place first. The front door was wide open—a bad sign. Inside was worse. I held my nose. "Eww." The smell of pee and puke, masked by disinfectant, was foul. And no one was at the front desk. Zero must-haves. So we left.

Then we moved on to the priciest place. We couldn't even get past the front door without signing in and showing some ID. A great sign. The place smelled like fresh flowers. The dining room had white tablecloths and a menu with names of foods I couldn't even pronounce. We toured rooms for books, movies, games—everything. Then our guide handed us the cost sheets. Mom's eyes bulged. And we left.

We spent the rest of the time at some in-between places—not so fancy and not too dumpy. Mom and Gran visited a few more homes during the week. They had tons of info, and each night I could hear them going over it in Gran's room. Though not a whiff about it left that room until the end of the week when Mom and Dad called everyone into the living room for the big reveal.

We now had new furniture in our living room. After the pop-up storm on Halloween, Mom said we needed at least one room that we weren't ashamed for people to see, whether we could afford it or not. Anyway, the new furniture was on the installment plan, just one more bill piling up on top of the others.

"You know," Mom said to Gran, "you need your own space." Then, like an MC hyping a huge press release, she scanned the room and gushed, "Thank goodness we've found a good fit." She clapped her hands together and cheered. "The Sunrise House!"

Gran winced. "Not interested," she said, then turned away and stared at nothing in particular that any of us could see.

Mom folded her hands in front of her. She took a deep breath and carried on, talking up Sunrise like it was some sort of adult Disneyland. "They have all kinds of activities. Movies, games, and—"

"I'm a Dancing Doll, not a bingo lady," Gran huffed.

Lines cracked across Mom's forehead. Tears welled in her eyes. "We've already talked about this," she said.

Gran tilted her head as if it were the first time she had heard anything about it.

It hurt my heart to see her disappearing like this, and I rushed over to hug her. "You'll be back over here all the time," I said.

"Yeah," Max said. He scrambled over and threw his arms around her middle.

Gran slumped over. All the puff pressed out of her like a deflating balloon. "For goodness' sake," she said with sad eyes, "I never thought I'd wind up in a Sunset House."

I squeezed her hand. "Sunrise House," I corrected gently.

Chapter 12

"Do you think you're in love?" Jen asked. "With Will or Shawn Mendes?" I laughed. Both were represented on my bedroom wall of hotties.

"Be serious or we're never going to fix this problem."

I swiped my hand in front of my mouth to wipe off the smile. "What if I am?"

Jen had come for another sleepover and an in-depth consultation on Will. I had written his name over and over in every section of my notebook, on my jeans, on my hands, on my Post-it wall. It was out of control. Worse, it was on display.

Max had seen the writing on my TWEEN board, and he wouldn't let me forget it. "Kattie likes Will, Kattie likes Will . . ." He would say it again and again in a low singsong voice just to drive me nuts.

Something had to be done. A sleepover was an

excellent start. When Jen arrived, the first thing we did was raid the fridge. We were in this for the long haul, so we had to fortify ourselves with enough food and drink for some heavy thinking. We stockpiled sodas, chips and salsa, cheese and crackers, two bags of candy corn, and some leftover pizza, carted it all up to my room, and slapped the "Do Not Disturb: Intruders Subject to Torture" sign on the door.

Jen had listened to the details of my situation. She was perched on my desk chair studying my wall, especially the mind-boggling number of Post-its with Will's name scribbled all over them.

"Hmm," she said.

"I'm going to need a lot more than *hmm*."

Jen munched on cold pizza for a while and downed some Coke. Then she leaned in close to where I was sitting on the edge of my bed. "For starters, you've got to talk to him. Be creative. Find a way to *accidentally*"—she air quoted— "run into him."

"Oh, I run into him all the time. You know . . . coming and going . . . at the bus stop."

"And what do you guys talk about?"

"Not much. I usually say 'hey.'"

"What does he say?"

"He says 'hi.' Sometimes he just nods."

"That's it?" She shook her head. "Well, you're going to have to do a lot better than that."

"Obviously."

Jen helped herself to some cheese and crackers and another swig of soda. She slumped back in the chair, propped her feet up on my desk, and went back into thinking mode. "Important ideas can't be rushed," she said.

I swiveled around, propped up my pillows against my headboard, and eased into them. Might as well be comfortable while her wheels were turning. I stared at my wall, the one half-covered with an almost life-size poster of my former crush, Shawn Mendes. Strange, I didn't even care about Shawn anymore. Besides—reality check—my chances with my celebrity crush were only just a fantasy.

I glanced at my other wall, the one with the TWEEN board and all the Post-its with Will's name scrawled on them. *Another fantasy? Maybe*. But my chances with the 3D hottie who lived right next door were way better than with any two-dimensional superstar. Plus, no poster ever made my heart race in my chest the way Will did every time I laid eyes on him. I didn't pull myself away from that TWEEN board until Jen sat upright and tossed out her idea.

"First off," she said, "we know he likes you."

My mouth fell wide open. "How do we know that?"

She gave me her *duh* look. "He compared you to the Good Witch of the North." She made one of her irritated *tsk* sounds at me. "*Soooooo*, today we launch our very own Spygate."

"You want me to become a creeper?"

"Please, you're not going to peek in his windows. You're just going to clock his movement every morning for a few days to pinpoint exactly when he leaves his house for the bus stop. Then you leave when he leaves." She flicked her wrist at me. "You can take it from there."

"Nice. Where should I take it?"

"Jeez, Kat, I don't know everything. I've never done this before. I've never even been in love."

"Okaaaay," I said. By then, I'd think of something to say, spontaneous or rehearsed, but casually delivered.

And guess what? It worked.

Chapter 13

William and I had taken the same school bus for months and had barely said a word to each other. Now in mid-November, nothing was quite as exciting as a walk to the bus stop together whenever we came out of our houses at the same time, which was often now that I was keeping an eye out for him. When Will stepped out of his house, I'd do a quick check of my reflection in the window, smooth any unruly piece of hair or rumpled clothing, and waltz casually out my door.

"Hi," I'd say.

"Hi yourself," he'd say.

Then we'd chatter away about everything, from schoolwork and teachers, to friends like Jen and Chip, or bullies like Maria and Luce. When we got to the bus stop, we'd split up and then Will would sit with Chip on the bus.

Today that changed, mostly because of

Romeo and Juliet. It was required reading for seventh graders. When we met up in front of my house this morning, I waggled my copy in front of him. "There are a few things that bother me in here."

"Like what?" Will asked.

I widened my eyes at him. "For one, do you really think a boy at a masquerade party, sort of like our Halloween party, would just march across the room to kiss a girl he doesn't even know in plain sight of everyone?"

He laughed. "I wouldn't."

"And she's ready to marry this Romeo guy the day after she meets him."

"Too fast for you?" he asked with a slight sound of amusement on his lips.

"Uh. Yeah," I clamored, bobbing my head up and down. "Especially since he's at her party to see another girl that he claims he's madly in love with."

Will creased his brow. "Do you think he's a player?"

"Maybe." I had a sneaking suspicion he might be poking fun at me for getting so fired up over this, but I pitched my bottom line anyway. "What's all the rush about?"

"Well," he suggested in a jokey kind of voice, "maybe they're so in love with each other that they can't think straight."

Point taken. I stared into his deep brown eyes with the gold flecks in them. Blushing, I looked down, then away.

By this time, we'd reached the bus stop. But we didn't separate.

Instead, Will spoke animatedly. "It's the parents," he said, windmilling his arms through the air to play up his words. "They cause a lot of problems with their stupid idea of an arranged marriage."

He dumped his backpack on the ground and pulled out his copy of the play. Then he flipped through the opening pages and pointed to the end of scene 1 where a fight broke out and the town leader jumped straight to the death penalty for anyone disturbing the peace.

He wrinkled his forehead. "If you ask me, all the *so-called* adults are out of control."

"What about those Capulet and Montague kids?" I tapped my finger on another place in scene 1 where the teenagers were fighting in the street, tearing up the town, ready to kill each other.

He gave me a slow, thoughtful nod. "A bunch of haters everywhere you look."

I tipped my head. "You know what, trash-talker Maria and her backup harasser Luce would fit right in with them."

"How about us?" Will asked. A mischievous grin spread across his face. "Where would we fit?"

Hmm. Was this simply a string of throwaway words rolling playfully off his tongue, or was he low-key hinting that we were, in some small way, like the star-crossed lovers in the play?

I had no words. Luckily, the school bus pulled up. "I'll have to get back to you on that one," I said over my shoulder as I boarded the bus.

I strolled down the aisle and took a window seat. Will was right behind me. He hesitated for a sec. Then, instead of moseying on back to sit with Chip like he always did, he swung in beside me. He smiled at me, and I smiled at him. It was goofy but romantic—and totally Romeo-and-Juliet-esque.

"Hey, Romeo," I whispered. The words just flew out of my mouth.

Uh oh, I thought. *Am I overplaying my hand?*

"Hey yourself, Juliet," he whispered back.

It was magical.

Occasionally, we'd get together after school. One Thursday afternoon, I watched Will pitch a baseball game. He was good, I mean *really* good. He was the only seventh grader ever to be named MVP of our junior baseball team.

Today, Will said that he was working on his off-speed pitches to complement his fastball and splitter. I didn't know the difference, but I sat in the bleachers gawking in awe at him as his blazing pitches zoomed into the catcher's mitt.

I brought a bag of cherries with me, and after practice, we sat there eating them, tossing the stems and pits back into the bag. The bright sunlight spilled over us, and fresh breezes blew around us—it was perfect.

The soft winds uncombed my long dark hair, and I twisted some of the loose-flying strands behind my ears. Then I questioned Will about his baseball wizardry.

"Do you think you'll go pro one day?" I asked.

"I don't know about that." Then he said that

his mom was pushing him to stick with baseball, and she thought it might pay off with a college scholarship. But anyone who'd seen the glint in his eye when he tossed one of his fastballs and the smile on his face when it zipped past the batter knew that it was a lot more than that. And when I raised a questioning eyebrow at him, he owned up to the real truth about it.

"I love baseball," he said, laughing. He lounged against the bleacher and soaked up the sun. He glanced over at me. "What do you think you'll do someday?"

I didn't dance around it like he had. Not even for a minute. "Easy one. I'm going to be a journalist," I said as if it were a calling as strong as a nun's. "Maybe a reporter for the *Albuquerque Journal*."

I loved my work on the school paper, but I longed for the day when I could work on a real story at a real newspaper, where an editor could put a stamp of approval on one of my tell-all stories that would go on to win the Writer of the Year Award. Lost in the dream, I sagged back on the bleachers and scooped up a bunch of cherries from the bag. "Though," I brooded, "I may not have a future if Maria doesn't get off my back." I laughed and slipped a cherry into my mouth.

"Tell her sticks and stones," Will said, squeezing my hand.

I turned into a gob of mush. I recalled when the swoon-worthy pirate charged in to rescue me from Maria's foul jaws at the Halloween dance. I sighed. "If only Jack Sparrow could always be there to save me from my tormentors."

He chuckled. Then he sat up. "Hey, you're hogging the cherries," he said, grabbing for the bag.

"I most certainly am not," I said, holding it just out of his reach.

He shoved his open palm forward with a single cherry cupped in it. "Then how come I only have one left?"

"I guess because you gobbled yours up, Mr. Piggy," I giggled.

He jerked his head back. "Are you calling me a pig?"

"If the shoe—"

Before I could finish, he flicked his cherry at me. It hit me in the face and startled me. He thought it was hilarious. He laughed and laughed.

I shrugged. "You think that's funny?"

"Yes," he said, laughing even harder.

"Good." With a poker face, I slid a handful of cherries mixed with pits and stems out of the bag and tossed it at him.

He squinched his eyes and frowned.

I couldn't help it. I started laughing hysterically.

He snatched the bag out of my hand, pulled out more of the messy mix, and threw it at me. I threw some back at him. We kept doing that until there was nothing left, all the while laughing our heads off. In the end, we collected the whole mucky mix of cherries, pits, and stems, tossed it in the trash can, and meandered our way home together as the sun faded from the sky.

When we got to my house, Will shuffled his feet and said, "Bye." But he didn't leave. He just stood there with his eyes fixed on the ground.

I fidgeted with my book bag and rattled my brain for something to say. Romeo and Juliet sprang to mind. "Hey, did you read the R and J balcony scene yet?"

He didn't answer me. He took a step closer until he was about two inches from me, so close that we were breathing each other's air. Then, gazing into my baby browns with his oh-so-fine eyes with gold flecks in them, he tilted forward and kissed me right on the lips. It wasn't a big kiss. His mouth was closed and the kiss was quick. But it was soft and sweet and PHENOMENAL. And it had come from Will.

He turned on his heels as if to leave, twirled back around, and said, "'Parting is such sweet sorrow.'"

So romantic.

Chapter 14

I t was Friday morning, and the late bell was already ringing when I dashed into my English class. The room was a full 360-degree panorama of photos of all the great writers we would read this year: Twain, Poe, Bradbury, Thurber, O. Henry, and a bunch more. One entire wall was devoted solely to Shakespeare and his *Romeo and Juliet*. So in this room, it was mostly hard to think about anything but English.

Not today.

I slid into my seat next to Jen. I'd already texted her that something mind-blowing had happened. I'd even hinted that it was a boy-girl thing. But I was pumped to actually share my head-rush news in person.

Mr. Garcia was a gem of a teacher with the knowledge and the knack. He even looked the part with his huge horn-rimmed glasses. He was mostly all business. But he was always open to questions, and there was room for laughter in his classroom. So I usually paid attention.

That didn't mean I was above taking advantage of his shortcomings. At times, he seemed oblivious to what was going on in his classroom. Things like talking didn't seem to faze him that much. Sometimes he would march up and down the aisles between the rows of desks as students whispered behind his back.

Mr. Garcia's golden rule was cell phones off in class, and I stuck to that. But he was on the move today, walking the aisles. I saw an excellent note-passing opportunity and grabbed it.

I pulled a sheet of paper from my notebook and scribbled on it.

My whole life has changed since yesterday. I think I'm in heaven.

I knocked the paper off my desk and watched it flutter to the floor.

Jen scooped it up and quickly scrawled something on it. Then she balled up the sheet and lobbed it over to my desk.

I smoothed out the crinkled paper and read her message: *Heaven? What did I miss?*

Then I wrote: *You missed what will go down as one of the most romantic moments of my life.*

I placed the note under a class worksheet and sneaked it over to her.

Jen wrote back. *Spill it.*

Just then, I glanced up and spotted Mr. Garcia's eyes on me. I pretended to be taking notes on whatever he was saying. I figured he fell for my act. Anyway, he redirected his attention to Billy Taswell, telling him to "lose the headset," which was turned up so loud that his music was filtering through to all of us. Of course, I should have stopped the note-passing then. But I needed to get my news out, so I waited until he turned his back.

I scrawled out my last note.

At exactly 5:16 late yesterday afternoon WILL KISSED ME.

I folded it into a paper airplane and winged it over to her.

My glowing revelation was in flight when Mr. Garcia snuck up from behind me and snagged it right out of the air.

"Kat Cruz," he called out. My name resounded throughout the room. He flattened the paper and held it out to me. "Read it," he demanded. "If it's that important, we'd all like to hear it." He hovered over me, his eyes drilling into me.

I could barely squeeze out one word. "No."

To him, it was a meaningless piece of trash. To me, it held the biggest secret of my life. The last thing I wanted was for anyone other than Jen to read it.

"Please move to a seat in front of the room," Mr. Garcia commanded in a sharp teacher-y voice.

Red-faced, I scooped up my books and obeyed orders, faking a look of control until I tripped over a backpack that was plopped in the aisle and almost tumbled to the floor. The best I could do after that was keep my head down and stumble to my desk, conspicuously followed by Mr. Garcia and surrounded by the giggles and smirks of some of my amused classmates.

Chip was one of those smirkers. He would probably tell Will. Could it get any worse? Maybe. The front seat I collapsed into happened to be next to Luce, bully-in-training to Maria. Her seat was just inches from the teacher's desk, where Mr. Garcia had carelessly tossed the note.

I caught Luce eyeing it and spent the rest of class scheming how I would nab it. When the bell rang, I went for it, but Luce slapped her hand down on it first. Good thing Mr. Garcia's prying eyes were on her.

"Is the note yours, Luce?" he asked.

She had no choice but to ditch it and leave.

I reached for it.

Mr. Garcia stopped me. "Let's lose the note, Kat."

I pivoted.

He was on to me, his hand outstretched.

I forked over the note.

Then, by some stroke of dumb luck, he glanced down and scanned the page. His icy look melted. "I can see from the huge capital letters that this was an important happening for you. Still, I am going to ask you to keep these breakthrough moments out of class." He paused, waiting for some response.

I turned as pink as a ham, and at that moment, I could not get my mouth to work.

"Unless you want to share them with all of us?" Mr. Garcia said.

I found the words. "No! No way," I said at top volume. "And never a peep from me about my personal life ever again." I jerked my thumb and forefinger clockwise in a circle to mimic that I would lock my mouth shut forever.

He turned and dumped the paper back on his desk.

Our convo was over, but my feet stuck to the spot. It was too soon to be opening my big mouth, but I wanted my note back. Really bad.

I pointed to his desk. "Mr. Garcia," I asked in a pip-squeak voice. "Can I *pleeeease* have that note?"

"What note?" he said and handed it to me.

I tossed it into my backpack and left before he could even think about changing his mind.

———

I finally dragged myself home that afternoon. So many things—good and not so good—had been happening all at once, and I needed some alone time to mull them over. I headed straight to my room and dumped everything out of my backpack, recovered the note, and tacked it up on my pink bulletin board. I stared at it, especially the WILL KISSED ME part, like forever. Actually, my life was pretty darn great. I just needed to keep it under wraps better.

I texted Jen: *Heads-up on the swiped note. WILL KISSED ME.*

Jen: *SHUT UP! Did Mr. G read it?*
Me: *Yep. Got it back.*
Jen: *Detention?*
Me: *Nope. Details later.*

I trotted off to the kitchen, where I was content munching on an Oreo and sipping some milk until I glanced over at my dad's laptop, which had a job-hunting site pulled up. Lately, my parents had been scouring for part-time jobs to make up for losses at the gym. I felt a twist in the pit of my stomach over it.

Then Max strolled into the kitchen with my note clutched in his hand. He was waving it in my face, chanting, "Kattie kissed Will, Kattie kissed Will..."

Color rushed to my cheeks. "Stay out of my room!" I hollered.

"The door was open," he said like that made it okay.

"So what?" I snapped.

"Soooooo," he sing-songed, puckering his lips and wagging the note gleefully in the air as if it were some prize for a game of marbles he'd won.

"Give it back."

"Or what?"

"Or else," I said, holding back on threats of a slow and painful death.

I should have thrown that note away. I should have torn it into a hundred-thousand itsy-bitsy pieces or torched it when I had a chance. But no, I'd posted it in plain sight on my wall. What was I thinking?

"Please, Max, give me the note. *Pleeeease.*" I couldn't believe I was reduced to begging.

"Hmm," he hummed.

I relaxed a teensy bit.

"Well, I'll think about it." He waggled his eyebrows and giggled.

Then I lost it. I took off after him. "I swear I will catch you and crush you like a midnight roach," I howled.

"Murder!" he yelled back at me in his don't-give-a-hoot tone of voice. He streaked across the room and flew through the front door. Too bad for him, he slammed smack into Dad.

Good, I thought. He'd been caught red-handed in the act with the note still gripped in his hand. Not even playing the baby card could get him out of this one.

I had managed to get my note back from Luce and my teacher, and I wasn't about to let my bratty brother have it. I didn't want Dad reading it either.

"It's mine! It's mine!" I screamed. "He stole it out of my room." Tears filled my eyes.

Dad could see how upset I was. Unlike Max, he knew I was almost a teenager, entitled to some privacy, and he took my side. He peeled the note from Max's fingers and gave it back to me without even looking at it.

"Max," he said, "you have your own room. Stay out of Kat's."

"B-but," sputtered Max, trying to worm his way out of it like he always did.

This time, Dad shushed him right up. "There are no *buts* in this." He crossed his arms and stood firm.

Max's smile drooped. He shrugged and said, "Whatever." But he slunk out of the room, dragging his feet.

Finally, Max got in trouble for something. I let out a huge sigh of relief, followed by a beyond-grateful look at my dad.

Chapter 15

Another Sunday afternoon meant another home improvement project. The focus was on my room this time. The paint color was pink, of course.

Max looked at the paint can and screwed up his face.

"What?" I asked.

"It's a girly color."

"And what am I?"

He gave me wide eyes and shrugged.

"Besides," I said, "a lot of boys like pink."

"Since when?"

"Since you fought like Superman to keep your pink hair on Halloween."

He giggled and got on with it.

During the week, Max had cut and pasted construction paper for a card. It had the name *Sue* on the front of it—*in glitter*. He'd wrapped some candy kisses in white tissue paper. He cinched his goody bag with a pink ribbon. It was sitting on top of the card near the front door of the house, ready to go the next morning.

Lately, Max and I had been working on the house together and chatting, so it didn't seem all that weird when I asked, "Who's Sue?"

"A girl," he said.

"Obviously. Do you like her?"

"Yes," he squeaked.

I waited a minute before asking, "What's in the card?"

Max squirmed and darted me a quick side-eye. Then he stopped painting, dropped his roller in the pan, and turned to face me. He planted his hands on his hips and tipped his head sideways, questioning me on it.

Our usual meaningless chatter was easy. Talking personal stuff was new. So, I shot him my most winning smile to loosen him up, and he fell for it.

"It's an *I'm sorry* card. I beat her at marbles. She said it wasn't fair 'cause I'm an expert. Now she won't talk to me."

"Oh," I said, wrinkling my brow like I was super concerned about it. "Should I tell her how much you like her?" I asked, thinking, *now maybe he'll see how mean he was to me at the Halloween party.*

Instead, he wailed like bloody murder. "NO!" He pan-dipped his roller for a fresh gob of pink, marched over to me, and painted a big stripe across the front of my sweatshirt.

I loved my weathered Grant Middle School sweatshirt. I hated the pink streak that now blocked out half of its brilliant red letters. Sure, I expected to get a rise out of Max, but I did not expect this. And I would not let it slide.

"Okay," I said. "Game on." I snatched up my roller, dipped it right into the can for an extra goopy roll, and painted a humongous stripe that stretched all the way from the top of his head down to his toes. "I hope the color pink is growin' on ya."

He squished up his whole paint-splattered face at me.

That was when Dad came to check on us. His eyes were wide as he stared at us. "You two look ridiculous."

Max and I took a peek in the full-length mirror on the back of my door. I was about to tell him how good he looked in pink, but I didn't want to stir things up anymore. Instead, we laughed at how silly we both looked.

Dad laughed with us for a sec. Then he slipped on his serious face. "You're not going to waste all of this good paint." He told us to get cleaned up and get back to work before Mom saw us.

We followed orders. I even helped Max get the gunk off his head. "You goof," I said, rustling his hair, and he giggled.

At the end of the day, it was a job well done together.

"I'm proud of you kids," Mom said.

Dad just smiled.

Gran came over that night for dinner and to check out my paint job.

Her settling in at Sunrise House had been bumpy. "It's a home for old people who can't remember anything," she'd grumbled in disgust over and over again, as if it wasn't the exact reason she was there.

Tonight, there was a break in that mantra. She was actually bubbling over, talking about a "lovely man" who'd whisked her out on the floor for some old-fashioned swing dancing during a social gathering earlier that day. She was almost giddy with the news, which left all of us a bit cheerier.

After we ate, I brought Gran upstairs for the big reveal of my room. With wide eyes, she scanned the whole room from the doorway. She came in and inspected the room, giving each wall a thorough looking over, from a distance and up close. Then she turned and looked at me, back at the walls, at me, the walls. She was making a big show of it, as if she were judging some prizewinning paint contest. It was funny, and I couldn't help laughing. But Gran was dead serious as she handed down her review.

"This is one beautiful red room."

I pitched my head to the side. "Pink, Gran." It was pink. Very, *very* pink.

"I know it's pink." She smoothed her skirt and went off on a rambling yarn about how my granddad had bought her a gorgeous red dress—fitted, cinched waist, low cut—and how she'd danced the night away in it.

I rolled with her dip into the past and pulled her back to me. "Well," I said. "How about dancing this night away?"

Gran refocused.

I showed her some steps from my Just Dance class, and she picked up every one of them. We were hip-hopping all over the place. I twirled her around, then she twirled me. We tried putting a few steps together for a routine, and they got all muddled. But who cared? We were having too much fun.

"Nothing's better than dancing with my daughter in a bright red room," Gran said.

I let it go this time and kept moving. I didn't know what else to do.

Chapter 16

I t was an unremarkable Saturday morning in December. I was polishing off a bran muffin and sipping some OJ, bored silly and wondering what I was going to do all day. Meanwhile, Max was wolfing down his Cheerios and throwing some at the dog, making a disgusting mess. Mom was studying her calendar and oblivious to it all, and Dad was reading the newspaper, just as oblivious.

From behind his *Albuquerque Journal*, Dad mentioned that a rare solar eclipse was coming to Albuquerque in March.

"Mmm," Mom said.

Then Dad said that the house down the street had been robbed. He lowered the paper to highlight the scariest part of the news. "When the Whitmores walked in on the guy, he pulled out a gun before making a run for it."

Mom's head snapped up. It was the first time we'd heard anything about a gun being used in one of these neighborhood robberies. Her forehead creased. "Any leads?"

Dad skimmed the article and reeled off a sketchy ID of a white male wearing torn jeans, a dirty T-shirt, and a ski mask.

I froze. *The creepy bag guy we saw on Halloween?* But lots of people wore all kinds of masks on Halloween. It didn't mean they were armed robbers out to terrorize the community. I glanced down at my ripped jeans and kept my mouth shut.

Dad shook his head and went back to reading.

Mom went back to her calendar.

I slumped over and let out a loud sigh.

Mom glanced up. "Are you up for some shopping?"

I did a double-take. "Yeah!"

Mom had decided I was old enough to be trusted with her charge card. The deal was that I would use the card to buy myself, and occasionally Max, a few things.

"I think it might be time," she said with a wink.

I had no idea what she meant. More quality time to spend with Max? And what was it with that wink?

"Time for what?" I asked.

She pulled me aside, out of earshot from Max and Dad. "Lately, I have been noticing that you are . . . filling out a little. Maybe it's time for a bra."

My eyes popped wide open. "Really?"

I'd been asking her about it ever since Jen got her first bra ages ago. Still, I looked down at my nearly flat chest. Could she see something that I missed? Whatever. I wasn't about to question her on it.

I couldn't wait to tell Jen. She was practically an expert on bras.

"We'll go bra shopping," Mom said. "I'll just go into the gym an hour later." Another wink. "Wouldn't miss it."

My day was shaping up and I was all smiles.

Then back at the breakfast table, Mom folded Max into the plan and my smile wilted.

"We'll take Maxie along," she said as if it was nothing at all. "He needs some new tennies, and there's a sale. You can help with that."

Max pumped his hands in the air. "Yippie! New shoes." Cheerio crud sputtered out of his mouth and dribbled down his Superman shirt. *Eww.*

"He can catch the next sale," I said, brushing off her shoe scheme.

Mom just zeroed in. "Maxie, show Kat your shoe."

Max held his shoe up in the air until it was staring me in the face. His big toe was poking through a hole in the front. Sure, it sucked to have sneakers with holes, but it wasn't the only thing that sucked.

I jabbed my finger at him, then whipped it up and down in the air from his head to his big toe that was sticking out of his shoe. "Look at him, Mom. He's showboating his whole breakfast."

"Oh, that tiny bit of spatter?" She scurried around the table with a napkin to polish him up. Then she stood back to admire her handiwork. "Ta-da! Perfection."

Not even close.

Max looked down at his drooling friend. "Moe comes too."

I cringed. Then I threw up my arms. "Okay. I'll lug Max along, but no way am I hauling that slobbering dog to the mall."

"Of course not, sweetie. Moe doesn't need any tennies." Mom chuckled at her wittiness. Then she tried to kiss me on the head like everything was just fine, but I twisted away from her. I was old enough to know when I'd been played.

I turned to Max. "We're leaving at ten. Be ready or we'll take off without you."

I tore up the steps to my room. I took a long look in the full-length mirror. I couldn't see much, but maybe my baggy sweatshirt was hiding my curves. I turned sideways and stretched my top skin tight. I could see something, but still not that much. I tore off the shirt and stared at my body.

"Yes!" I said with a fist pump. "They are growing—not a lot, but some." The breast bumps were clearly bigger. I jiggled them and noticed a subtle bounce. Mom was right. *I'm ready for a bra!*

At exactly ten o'clock, we headed out for the mall in our clunky SUV. Fifteen minutes later, we approached the lingerie department at Macy's.

"Can I help you?" a smiling gray-haired saleslady asked.

I spoke up with confidence. "Yes," I said. "I need a bra. Size 30A, please."

Mom cupped her hand under her chin, sizing me up. "Let's try a few—30A, maybe 30AA." The saleslady helped us gather them, and I skipped off to the dressing room with Mom.

"Now you sit right here, Maxie," Mom said as she pointed to the bench just outside the dressing room door. "Don't move an inch. If you're good, Kat will take you to get some new shoes. You understand?"

"Fine," Max said, and he plopped down on the bench.

First, I tried on an A-cup bra. Despite the obvious fact that my boobs were growing, they were still not big enough to fill the A-cup space. The puckered cups looked as wrinkled as the distress lines on my forehead. I ripped that bra off and tried on another A-cupper. Worse. I frowned and tugged it off too.

Mom twisted her mouth. "I'm afraid those A-cut bras won't work."

I grabbed one of the AA-cup bras. Mom and I fiddled and fidgeted with the hooks and straps, adjusting everything just as I had seen Jen do with her first bra. Then I leaned forward and stuffed every bit of my tiny boobs into those small cups. I checked myself out in the mirror from every angle possible. I turned to Mom. She okayed it with a big smile and a nod of her head.

Mom poked her head out to check on Max. Then she came back in and eagle-eyed me, tightened the straps, and pinched at the sides. She twirled me around for a check on the back and the cups. She stepped away and carried out a final overview.

"Perfect!" she said with a full-blown grin.

Yay! I waltzed out of the dressing room—head and bra held high—and plunked my AA-cupper down on the counter.

Mom smiled at me. "I need to get to work. You can pay for your bra, then take Maxie to get some shoes. Please get him something practical. I'll see you at home."

I hugged my mom, and then she set off.

I rifled through my purse for my charge card, feeling like a total adult.

Just then, someone snuck up from out of nowhere and snatched my bra right off the counter. Startled, I spun around to face the two biggest bullies on the planet.

"OMG! It's an AA cup," Maria squealed, holding my bra up on display.

My face turned as red as a beetroot.

"Hardly a bra at all," Luce laughed.

When I grabbed for it, Maria tossed it back on

the counter. "Don't worry. I don't need a training bra."

My entire body tensed.

"Girls," the saleslady intervened. "Can I help you with something?"

"No thanks. We're here for the shoe sale," Luce said.

"That way to shoes," the saleslady said stiffly, pointing to the left.

Unfortunately, when the mean girls turned that way, Max was standing there with the bra draped over his shoulders, the cups dangling in front of his Superman shirt. He placed his hands on his hips, puffed out his chest—and bra cups—and grinned.

Maria and Luce laughed like loons.

"Looks like they wear the same bra size," Maria sniggered over her shoulder on the way to the shoes.

Max's chest deflated and his frown matched mine.

"Fresh as salt, those girls," the saleslady said with a frown.

I blushed, undraped the bra from Max's front, paid for it, and darted out of there as fast as I possibly could. Outside, I sucked in a deep breath of fresh air. Then I let it flow slowly from my lungs to drum out Maria's bad vibes. *Better.*

I glanced down at Max. I really couldn't be mad at him for checking out a bra after I'd left him surrounded with nothing but bras.

"Shoes?" I asked, smiling down at him.

"Shoes." He giggled, ready to march back into Macy's.

"Oh no," I said, catching his hand. The shoe department at Macy's was off-limits. I didn't care if it was the sale of the century or how strapped for cash my family was because there was no way I was setting myself up for another run-in with the mean girls.

"We're going to a *real* athletic store for *big-boy* shoes."

"Okay!" Max whooped, and we high-fived on it.

Max tried on a whole bunch of shoes. He was so amped up about the Nike Airs that he didn't want to take them off. Of course, we couldn't bring them back to the store if he wore them home, and Mom might not be wild about the new shoes or the coin we dropped on them. But Max's ginormous smile as he checked them out every which way was priceless. All things considered, I figured what the heck.

Max left Dick's Sporting Goods wearing shoes that were way better than his old ones. And I had my very first bra. All in all—despite two evil bullies—not a bad day for the Cruz kids.

Chapter 17

S oon after the Whitmore burglary, Principal Gray's booming voice over the PA system encouraged all Grant Middle School students to be on the lookout for any strangers hanging around school who might be the neighborhood thief. "Say something if you see something," he said.

I went straight to Ms. Ramirez. She agreed with me that kids could be at risk and that the *Grantline* should cover the story. I banged out my warning.

BE AWARE

A burglar is on the loose in our school district. He is armed and dangerous. So far, he's broken into homes. But kids are probably not immune from his attention because he likes iPhones and laptops a lot. He's middle-aged, white, average build, and wears grubby clothes—ripped jeans and a dirty tee. His ID is skimpy because he wore a ski mask in his break-ins. He could be your neighbor, a guy living on the street, or someone hanging out at the mall or a fast-food place. If you see anything suspicious, call the police or report it to us at the *Grantline Newsletter.* DO NOT CONFRONT HIM.

Remember, you are our eyes and ears. If you see something, say something, and we'll check it out. A tip box will be set up in the main office.

We didn't expect much of a response, but the next day the tip box was overflowing. I immediately called an emergency meeting for the Grantline staff. We all gathered in the conference room, ready to bust open the case that no one else could solve. We dumped the mountain of notes onto the big round table in the center of the room and dug in.

Ruby read the first note. "Spotted a young guy outside school who looked like he should be inside if he cleaned up his knotted hair and filthy clothes."

"Too young to be our thief," I said.

DJ read the next note. "A shady-looking old man hanging out at the McDonald's down the street gave me an ugly sneer just for staring at him." He stopped reading. "Not enough to go on here," he said.

We read every single note. Unfortunately, our tips mostly ID'd a bunch of delinquents and loiterers near our school or at the local strip malls. Some of the ne'er-do-wells had straggly hair and raggedy clothes. Others had taunting looks or shifty eyes. But not one of them had a history of stealing anything or threatening anyone with or without a gun.

The entire *Grantline* staff agreed there was not one solid burglar sighting in the lot. But as a serious journalist covering an important story and the editor of our paper, I thought it might be smart to turn our stack of tips over to the police. Maybe with all of their resources, they would catch something that we had missed.

Two days later, the police returned our stack of notes with one of their own: Thanks, but no thanks. CREDIBLE LEADS ONLY.

I read it and blinked. I'd expected to be applauded as a promising newswoman of the future. Instead, I was dismissed as a downright amateur.

Principal Gray pulled the tip box from the office counter.

It was a big *L* for the *Grantline* and me.

Chapter 18

My Just Dance class had wrapped up, and I was itching to go home. At around six, Mom usually drove Max and me home for dinner, but she was tied up with gym business. I didn't want to hang around and neither did Max. So we were two antsy kids standing at the front sign-in desk, where Mom was tallying up end-of-month membership accounts.

"Done soon," she said. "Use the machines or take another class." She twisted her hair into a topknot and dug back into the accounts.

Our gym had a room full of treadmills, Stairmasters, rowers, bikes, and two classrooms in the back—one for barre, Zumba, and Just Dance (my fave), and another with mats and weights for yoga, Pilates, and BodyPump. There was also a kids' room with a small jungle gym and slide, a shelf full of books for reading and coloring, and a box overflowing with toys.

I slipped into a yoga class for some stretching,

and Max padded back to the kids' room to wrap his body every which way around the bars of the jungle gym.

An hour later at seven o'clock, we were back at the front desk and Mom was still crunching numbers.

"I'm hungry," Max whined.

I did some quick finger-tapping on my watch. "We're off," I said.

Mom looked at us with questions in her eyes. She slurped her smoothie and thought about it. She would never send Max home alone at night in the dark.

"You know I'm his almost full-time babysitter and the only one taking care of him a lot of the time," I said. "I don't even know why you're concerned about it."

"Okaaaay," Mom said, "but don't talk to strangers and don't dawdle."

"Mom, it's only half a mile." I rolled my eyes at her, and we were out of there.

About halfway home, I stooped down to tie my shoelace. When I straightened up, Max was staring at the houses across the street. All the homes on this block looked the same: two-story, white stuccos with red clay roofs, arched entryways, and shallow porches. Kind of cute. But we passed them all the time. I didn't get why he was so fixed on them now.

"Whatcha lookin' at?" I asked.

"The man on the porch," he said, pointing at the house right in front of us.

Usually, I would have said *so what* and walked on by, but a robber had been prowling the neighborhood. Plus, I was an up-and-coming reporter who'd written an article about it, and Max was a wannabe superhero. So we took a closer look. We stretched our necks and squinted our eyes, but it was hard to see much. The house was completely dark, and there was no streetlight or moonlight. All I could make out was a guy peeping in the front window. I saw him tug at it. Then he moved to the front door and rattled the knob.

Max and I looked at each other. *Is it the Crystal Park burglar?*

Obviously, I smelled something fishy. But I didn't want to go crazy about it and stick my nose where it didn't belong.

"Come on," I whispered.

Quietly, we crept to the other side of the street and crouched down behind a car. We inched our heads up and saw through the car windows that the man on the porch was still fiddling with the doorknob. I bent down and rummaged through my backpack for my iPhone. I dialed 911.

"What's your emergency?" the operator asked.

"Someone's breaking into a house," I said in a loudish whisper.

"Who's there?" called out the man on the porch in a grumbly sort of voice.

I was totally spooked. I grabbed Max's hand and lost my grip on the phone. I could hear it smashing on the ground. Still, I never looked back, not once. I just ran, pulling Max with me. We flew down the street, darted between cars, and whizzed around corners until we got home. We were both shaking. Max was crying.

"We're safe, we're safe," I kept telling him. I put my arms around him. He calmed down, and I called the gym. My parents phoned the police and came rushing home. The first thing they did was hug the daylights out of us and made sure we were okay.

Meanwhile, a police car pulled up to our house with its lights flashing and siren blaring. Two police officers were ushered into the living room. One of the officers pulled a notepad from his back pocket. His face turned deadly serious. "We're going to need a detailed description."

"Uh. It was dark," I said.

The officer turned to Max.

Max wrinkled his face and shrugged.

"Next time anything like this happens, I'll keep my eye on the details," I mumbled.

"My God," Mom said. "I certainly hope there's not a next time."

"There better not be," Dad said.

Just then, the officer got a call from the crime scene. Apparently, there'd been no burglar. It was the homeowner. He'd locked himself out and was searching for a way into his house.

"Oh," we all said with big, surprised eyes.

"Kids," Dad said to the officer.

"Children," said Mom.

I did not appreciate being talked about as if I were an irresponsible child. I was grown up enough to take charge and get myself and Max out of what could have been a high-risk spot. Why wasn't I getting any credit for that? Sure, I'd gotten caught up in the moment and was overly suspicious of the man on the porch. But the entire town was on edge.

Sad to report, the police found my phone at the scene. The screen had been shattered to smithereens. *Ugh.*

My parents thanked the officers for their time. We followed them outside and stood on the lawn to watch them drive off. The loud whoop of their siren had alerted our neighbors. Some peeked out of their windows. Others came patrolling.

"Was there a break-in?" asked Mr. Barlow, rushing over to us with his face all rumpled in concern.

"No. False-flag burglar alert," Dad said, brushing aside the full story.

Mrs. Morris shook her head and babbled on about how we were "gonna catch the guy" and how "he'd better not show his face around here again." Finally, she ran out of steam, turned, and gave an all-clear signal to our eavesdropping neighbors, even though there'd been no burglar.

We all gladly called it a night.

Chapter 19

"You are the birds and the bees," crooned Lulu, the newest teacher at Cruz's Athletic Club. Lulu arrived in mid-January all the way from New York City. She brought with her a new kind of exercise class called Dance Party. A fad in New York but unseen in Albuquerque, my parents hoped it would catch fire and pay off. They promoted the heck out of it. I was psyched about learning some new dance moves. But when I showed up, my mom said it was strictly for adults.

I peeped in at the class anyway when Mom wasn't around. There was something about it that kept me glued to it from the minute I heard Lulu shout, "Lift those butt cheeks higher, ladies!" Yes, she really said that and a whole lot more.

"Don't just walk around. Strut like a peacock!" Lulu stuck out her chest and backside to demo, then she strutted her stuff like nobody's business.

And later, "Raise those chins up. Show the whole world you mean it." Her voice pulsated throughout the room. *"At-ti-tude!"* she called, pounding out each syllable with a thump of her stomping foot.

Lots of giggles followed each of Lulu's calls. At the same time, her students held their chins a touch higher. And they circled with a springier step. *They had attitude.*

I was hooked. Dance Party was full of jazzy hip rolls and body shakes like our gym's Just Dance class that I loved, but with a happening fresh twist. Definitely the newest thing out there, and I knew I was going to be the coolest kid in school when I performed at the Grant's Got Talent Show in February. I talked to Lulu, and she agreed to help me with some of the moves.

Lulu was one of a kind. She had blue gel-spiked hair and used what she called "stage-ready makeup," a lot of dark eye shadow and fire-engine-red lipstick. She wore a plain black leotard, black tights, and red high heels. I could hardly take my eyes off her when she was danc-ing. I wanted to have that effect on my audience, especially Will.

I slipped into fantasyland just thinking about

the awesomeness of it. I pictured myself dancing under bright stage lights with the eyes of a packed house riveted on me. When I finished my routine, the audience would erupt and clap with all of its might. Then a boy, with deep brown eyes with golden flecks sprinkled in them and sandy curls of hair brushing his brows, would gift me a lush pink rose.

"Ready?" asked Lulu.

I blinked and slid back to reality.

That Friday after school, I took a lesson with Lulu while Mom was out of the gym taking care of bank business and picking up supplies.

"Your parents are okay with this, right?" asked Lulu just before we started.

"They're busy," I said. "But the school auditions all the acts, and they're total puritans."

Lulu laughed, and we got down to it.

We worked on a lot of swivels—forward, back, left, right—and "all-around-the-world moves," as she called them. We moved around the dance floor, adding dips, kicks, and wiggles to our choreographed routine.

Lulu didn't just give me a quick demo. She coached me on every step. "All the way, Kat! Extend your leg and point your toe!" If I just slightly rolled my hips, she shouted, "Bigger, bigger, Kat!" And she always instructed, "With attitude! It's not a good performance without attitude."

She helped me string together a routine with the right number of kicks, turns, and wiggles to fill the music and *wow* the crowd. I needed practice, but basically, I was good to go. I patted myself on the back for thinking outside the box and counted down the days until my performance.

Chapter 20

T he Valentine's Day cards were everywhere, set on desks, tucked into books, taped to lockers. Candy, too, especially the multicolored hearts and chocolate kisses. Exchanges were for everyone—girlfriends and boyfriends, regular old friends, teachers. Jen and I swapped cinched bags of heart candies, the same as every year.

But this year, V-Day was even more special on account of my *almost*-boyfriend. Will and I weren't really dating, and we definitely weren't going steady. We barely saw each other at school—not in class, not at lunch, usually not even after school. Still, we sat on the bus together, but we'd only shared that one kiss. We were more than buddies, which led me to the question I'd been stressing about all week long: Should I expect a Valentine from Will?

Jen said "yes," sort of. On Valentine's Day morning, she said that I would "for sure" get something from Will. In the afternoon, she pared it down to "probably." After school, she switched it to "maybe." Time was running out, and I had all but given up when I straggled home and spotted it tied to the porch railing.

It was the biggest balloon I'd ever seen. And believe me, I wasn't the only one who thought so. My parents, the Barlows next door, really anyone on the street who poked a nose out the door couldn't miss the big balloon with its red ribbon sashes fluttering in the breeze. There was a red rose inside the balloon, and it took my breath away. The note attached was a simple one: To Kat, From Will. But *wow* did it blow my mind. And it put the biggest, goofiest grin on my face until I realized that I hadn't done anything nearly good enough for him. In a flat second, my bliss burst like a popped balloon.

Earlier that week, I had cut out a big red heart from construction paper. The white letters I pasted on it said, "Have a Happy V-Day." Simple and sincere. But now that silly homemade pasteup wasn't going to measure up.

I knew I absolutely had to find *at least* a card with the right message for him. Emergency-style, I called Jen and she rushed over. Then we scrambled over to the Hallmark store in search of the best card I could find on such short notice. I mean, this wasn't like a Christmas card that was good for a whole season or a birthday card that could be belated. Valentine's Day was only one day with a clear-cut expiration date on it.

We stood in front of the card rack, debating. Nothing seemed quite right. The innocent kitten and puppy dog cards were for elementary school kids. The promises of love cards were for the adults. None of the *I Love You* cards worked for me. Fun and friendly was all I wanted. But I didn't see any good ones.

"How about a stuffed animal or a box of chocolates?" Jen said, trying to stay positive.

I browsed those shelves. Nothing on them was cheap, and I only had ten dollars burning a hole in my pocket. The cards alone were four and five dollars each.

"Too pricey," I told Jen.

"Well, here's something unique," Jen said, still upbeat. "The Legend of Saint Valentine." She held up a card with a full page of gold script about the Christian martyr Valentinus, who wouldn't go along with the Roman Emperor's wish to worship a bunch of gods. He stuck with Christ and was imprisoned and slaughtered, but not before encouraging a blind girl to believe so strongly in his God that her sight was restored.

Jen tapped her hand over her heart and read the end of the story to me. "The night before his death, on February fourteenth, he wrote a note to the girl and signed it: 'From your Valentine.' She planted an almond tree near his grave as a symbol of their friendship, and now similar messages of love are exchanged around the world on this day." She grinned her approval.

I wasn't feeling it. "Touching." I pulled a face. "But too historical. I need it to be more personal. And simpler."

"Well, if that's all you want, I have found *the* card," she said. She snatched it from the rack and handed it to me. "Hugs and Kisses to You on Valentine's Day." The cover had a tic-tac-toe grid on it with *x*'s and *o*'s in all the boxes. There was a heart-shaped happy face in the center with glittery sparkles.

"You're brilliant," I said. "Simple and sweet." I shrugged. "Best available, anyway."

I eyed the candy counter again, in particular the boxes of oversized candy kisses still available on the shelf. The card alone wasn't really enough.

But coupled with a giant four-by-four-inch chunk of chocolate, it might be.

I scooted over and snapped it up. "A kiss in a box!" I squealed.

"Perfect!" Jen squealed back.

The kiss-card combo was a done deal.

I gave Jen a hug for her help, paid for the stuff, and sprinted home in time to deliver my gift, text Will about it, and gleefully fly my balloon from out of my bedroom window. I knew Will could see it from his window while he chowed down on his candy.

Turned out to be an extra-special Valentine's Day after all.

Chapter 21

A kiss here, a kiss there, and a couple of weeks later, after another walk home from school, Will and I shared *a romantic moment in time*.

I'd stayed after for my weekly *Grantline* meeting, and Will had stayed after for baseball. I was working on an editorial in response to a lame letter from the PTA moms who were calling for a dress code at school. Ms. Ramirez had approved my editorial. She said she thought it was time. But there was still a sticking point.

The new president of the PTA and chief letter writer was Lily Morris, no one other than Will's mother. *An unfortunate turn of events.* So I thought I'd better run my editorial by Will before publishing.

We met up in front of the school, and I handed him the PTA's letter. "Please read the first line out loud," I said.

He nodded. "Our children are shamelessly

baring their bodies for public viewing." His cheeks flushed. *So, he was familiar with the quote.*

I pointed to a highlighted line. "Read here."

"The girls' short shorts are too short, their miniskirts are disgracefully skimpy, and their skinny jeans are too tight," he said.

I tapped his hand to stop him there. "What would you say if I didn't agree with your mom in my editorial?"

He threw up his hands in a sort of hands-off position. "Hey, freedom of speech for all."

So far, so good. But I wasn't finished. "Now read here."

He hesitated, but I drummed my fingers on another highlighted passage, motioning for him to go on.

"The boys are no better. Some of their jeans are too baggy and loose, sometimes slipping down their hips to expose their underpants," he read.

I looked him right in the eyes. "What did you say to your mom about *this*?"

He handed the letter back to me. "I pick and choose my battles with her."

I skimmed the letter to appear kind of preoccupied and less pushy with my question. "Did she ever bring up this dress-code thing to you?"

"Sort of," he said. He twisted his body, uneasy again.

I just smiled and waited for him to say more.

He wavered, then said, "She busted Chip for being a loose-jeans guy."

"Oh," I said, acting all surprised, even though I really wasn't. Chip always wore his pants hanging halfway down his butt with his underwear on full display, and not always the cute baseball-bat boxer kind either. "What'd you tell her?" I asked.

"I told her to leave my friends out of it."

Good answer. To firm it up, I pulled a copy of my editorial from my backpack and read the opening line to him. "The PTA—made up of moms with obvious links to Puritan times or possibly the Ice Age—is dead set against middle-schoolers making a modern-day fashion statement."

"Tough review," he said.

I nodded. "Uh-huh." Then I read another line. "Newsflash PTA Moms: miniskirts, short shorts, and skinny jeans are some of today's looks, and the old Bedrock era looks are never coming back."

"Maybe lose the Bedrock comp. Slightly less offensive."

I got the hang of Will's more diplomatic vibe. I didn't want to totally kill the editorial's punch, but maybe I could dial it back and scrap the Ice Age and Bedrock references.

"Mm," I said. "Okay. I get it. I'll soft-soap my jabs at the PTA."

"Good call," he said, and we moved on.

Walking home, we passed the strip mall where Gran had lost her way home, the Macy's where Maria had held my bra hostage, the white stuccos where Max and I had almost tangled with an imagined burglar and arrived at my porch where Will and I had our first kiss.

As usual, I didn't want to let Will go. "How about a snack?" I asked.

"Sure," he said. "If there's no dress code."

"Cute," I said.

We strolled through the front door and headed for the kitchen. We grabbed a few protein bars and sodas and moved to the small family room next to it. The TV and my mom's CD player were there. I didn't think twice about it until Will tripped on one of the uneven floorboards on the way to the sofa. Then I saw it. The room was a wreck. One wall had nearly caved in, and the other three had cracks in them. Plus, the floor was an obstacle course. I had tuned it all out, but it was hard for an outsider to ignore.

I cringed. Why hadn't I taken him to the living room? The floor was all one level there, and the furniture was brand new.

I could feel my face flushing. "This room's a fixer-upper," I said.

"Not *so* bad," he said.

We sank down on the soiled sofa and dumped our snacks on the stained coffee table. On the opposite wall, plaster, paint, and tools were staring us in the face.

"Need some help with it?" he asked.

"Sure," I said. "Sunday afternoon. Any Sunday afternoon."

We settled back into the cushions. Mom, Dad, and Max were at the gym. So we were all alone, feeling really cozy on the sofa, sipping sodas and munching on our bars, when Will scooched over closer to me. He leaned in and kissed me.

Every kiss with Will was magical. We'd had

them before. But this one stood out because another one followed. First, there was a peck of a kiss—sweet, then a real one—tingly and TOTALLY NEW. My heart was flipping and flopping all over the place. And all I could think was—SPELLBINDING.

Unfortunately, that was when we heard the jangling of my mom's keys at the front door, an impossible mood buster.

"Hi, kids," Mom said, arching a brow as she passed by us.

Max ran over and grabbed a treat from the coffee table.

The spell was one hundred percent broken.

Will left soon after that, and I bounded up the stairs to my room two at a time, smiling all the way.

Chapter 22

It was Sunday afternoon. And could you believe it? Will showed up in an old sweatshirt and jeans, ready to paint. When he knocked on our front door, Dad answered before I could get there.

"I'm afraid Kat can't come out to play right now," Dad said.

I slid in front of my dad and pulled Will into the living room. "Will's here to help. Do you have a problem with that?"

"No," Dad said with wide, surprised eyes. He smiled and waved Will toward the family room.

The room was prepped and ready to go. New drywall had replaced the collapsing wall, and mesh and plaster covered the mishmash of cracks and holes in the other three walls. The paint was set out. Mom, Dad, Max, and I each took our places in front of a wall. Will stood on the perimeter, sizing up the scene.

"I'll just slip in here next to Max," he said. He

grabbed an extra roller, moved a small half ladder from the middle of the room next to Max, and put the paint pan on it. He twirled Max around, wriggled his hands under his arms, and lifted him just a little bit off the floor to test his weight.

Max giggled.

"Ready?" Will asked.

"Uh-huh."

Will flexed his muscles, nothing compared to my weight-trainer Dad's but still impressive. This time he hoisted Max all the way up over his head and onto his shoulders.

Max steadied himself.

"Okay," Will said to him. "We're a team. You paint the top. I'll paint the bottom. And let's see whose wall gets finished first."

Max gazed at his competition—Dad, Mom, and me, all bigger than him with longer arms for painting. Taller, too, with a higher reach.

Still, Max would not back down. He scanned the room one final time, then grinned his I've-got-this grin. He rolled his paint and yelled, "Go!"

It was a real nail-biter for a while with Max falling narrowly behind. But he zeroed in, putting all of Dad's past instruction to the test. He gobbed as much paint on his roller as he possibly could.

His strokes were long and even. And he kept going, even when the rest of us took breaks. Plus, he had those two extra arms working for him. Was it the extra arms he had or the extra breaks we took? I didn't know. The only sure thing was that Max and Will wrapped up first. No contest.

"Excellent job," Dad said, ruffling Max's mop of hair.

Max beamed. We all did. It was the most fun we'd had painting the place, and it was all thanks to Will.

I couldn't stop smiling about it.

Chapter 23

My parents knew about the talent show. They said they'd be too tied up at the gym to come. What else was new? It was what I expected, and what I counted on.

Then, out of the blue on the night of the show, they called from the gym and sprung it on me that they were coming. They'd be late and would pick up Gran on the way. To save time, they wanted to know if I could take Max with me instead of dropping him off at the gym.

First of all, I had a suspicion my dance might be too grown up for my parents. And how was I supposed to get in the zone saddled with Max on my big night? But what could I do? He was seven. I couldn't leave him home alone.

I grabbed a duffel bag with my gear in one hand and Max's hand in the other, and we walked over to the school. Mom and Dad were still MIA when we got to the auditorium. So I sat Max on a stool on the side of the stage where I could keep an eye on him and he could watch the show.

Then I heard the stage manager yell, "Places!" I tore off my jeans and sweatshirt, tossed them into the sack, and took my spot in the lineup.

The acts were a mixed bag, everything from an Elvis impersonator who was "All Shook Up," to a baton twirler who kept dropping her baton, to a gymnast who did amazing jumps and twirls on a four-inch balance beam, to Will and Chip—who were set to play guitar and sing. I was performing right after them, so they were standing in front of me.

"Kickin' outfit," Chip commented.

I couldn't tell if he meant it or was messing with me. "Thanks," I said, keeping it simple. I refused to let anyone ruin my good vibe.

Then Will and Chip were up. They delivered a version of "Hallelujah" to make your heart melt. And that last "hallelujah" note, with Will's eyes shining in the stage lights, took my breath away. They got a lot of applause.

After that, I went on. I was the last act.

"Crush it," Will said, holding up his thumbs.

I smiled at him as I took the stage. I was a bundle of nerves at the same time that I was confident about my performance. Mostly, I just wanted Will to like it.

I wore stage-ready makeup like Lulu's, a black leotard and tights, and red cowboy boots as my costume. My music was Katy Perry's "Waking Up in Vegas," one of my mom's favorite songs that I didn't think she'd mind me using for my performance. My dance was a cute jazzy routine, a lot like my Just Dance class numbers, but with the new moves Lulu had taught me.

I took center stage, and the spotlight was shining on me. The music played, filling the auditorium. I started with small moves. Then I channeled Lulu—*All the way, Kat! Bigger, bigger! Swish those hips around the whole wide world! And do it with at-ti-tude!* I let loose, twisting and twirling on a show-stopping high.

As far as I could tell, the audience was rapt. Most of the time there was barely a sound. Of course, there were move-specific reactions. When I hit the beat with an especially hard hip pop, I heard a few *oohs* from the crowd. Once when I threw a particularly strong body pump, I heard a couple of *aahs*. I was in the zone as I strutted across the stage in my red boots, channeling the real Lulu attitude. Toward the end of my dance, when I shook my body to the beat of the music, a group of students moved up pretty close to the stage and gave me some cheers. I took it all as a positive. That was until I heard a collective gasp and a burst of laughter from one part of the crowd. There were claps too. So, I figured it was a mixed review.

The curtain fell, and all the performers joined friends and family in the auditorium lobby for punch and cookies. Mom, Dad, and Gran had arrived just after the performances started. I found them at the refreshment table with Max and Jen.

"Well," I asked, "what did you think?"

"That was fire!" Jen raved.

She had come with me to audition it a few weeks ago when no one was particularly shocked by it. Of course, tryouts had been without the costume, music, or the real Lulu attitude.

"How did you come up with that dance?" Dad asked.

Mom looked horrified and didn't beat around any bushes. "Those gasps and laughs you heard were from the parents in the crowd who thought your dance was inappropriate for a girl your age."

"I thought it was fine . . . cutting edge."

"That song? Those moves?" Mom questioned. "That was too mature for a child's dance."

I put my hands on my hips, planted my feet, and let her know for the record, "I am not a child, thank you very much."

"Oh?" Mom said.

"No," I said, whipping my hand up and down my body. "I am every inch almost a teenager."

Mom scoffed. "*Almost*," she shot back. She steamed for a bit. Then she really took off. "Until you're grown up enough to exercise better judgment, this is the last time you do anything in public that isn't approved by me and rubber-stamped by your father." She paused for a minute and took a breath, but she still wasn't finished with me. "I just hope the whole community doesn't judge us all because of this."

That stung.

Not any way to treat talent, but I wasn't counting on any big turnaround from Mom. I turned my back on her and faced Gran. "Dancer to dancer, what did you think?" I asked, hoping against some odds that she'd even remember my act.

Gran tossed me a devilish smile and told me that I shouldn't worry about what the audience thought because it was packed with old fuddy-duddies who didn't know good showmanship when it was staring them in the face. She placed her hands on my shoulders and said, "You, my young lady, are a regular Dancing Doll."

A grin stretched from ear to ear, and I gave her a big ol' bear hug of thanks. Grans were treasures, especially the dancing kind. Plus, mine almost always took my side.

She swiveled her head around and gave Mom a sharp look. "Ease up, Dot. You know Dance Party is just another exercise class."

Mom didn't seem convinced. "Not for a twelve-year-old," she repeated. She shot me one final dagger before she tromped off.

Gran shrugged. "I'm going to go find your grandpa."

"Gran . . ." I started to correct her, but she was already moving away and mixing in with the crowd. I saw her latch onto Dad, so I knew she was okay. But scary stuff.

Just then, Will drifted over to chat.

Not a minute later, Mrs. Morris swung by.

"We're leaving now," she told him without even saying hello to me.

Will raised his hand in an apologetic half-wave goodbye, and off they went.

I checked my phone for more feedback. Maria had posted a tweet, calling my performance "classless." *Typical.* I showed it to Jen, and she posted her own tweet, calling my dance "classy."

Even better, I got a text from Will saying that my act was "in a class all by itself." My heart leaped. He liked it. That was good enough for me.

Chapter 24

Practically overnight, everything changed.

It had never been my intention to bring down the family business. I actually thought my routine would be good PR for Cruz's Athletic Club and that everyone would be signing up for Lulu's class in droves the next day. Some did, but others had a negative reaction. The Crystal Park gym bunch, led by none other than Lily Morris, found my dance in "bad taste." They complained to the school for not "fully previewing" my act, and they wanted our gym to cancel the "indecent" exercise class.

Mom and Dad were all over me about creating hard feelings in the community and putting them in a tricky position. Dad said that if they kept the class, Lily's crowd would probably leave the gym. But Mom argued that if they dropped the class the ladies who loved it might leave.

In the end, my parents decided that the class

was *not indecent* and that it was way too popular to scrap. Of course, Mrs. Morris and her friends no longer came to our gym, and there was a cool wind blowing between our two houses.

No one was there when I bounced out of the house for school the morning after Mom and Dad decided to keep the Dance Party class. I sat on the porch steps, waiting for Will to roll out of his house.

I slipped my cheapo phone from my backpack to check my messages. Yeah, my parents had bought me a horse-and-buggy level phone so I could keep in close touch when I had Max with me. I took a good look around. If Maria saw the phone, it would probably go viral.

A text from Will said: *Mom's driving me to school.*

I texted back: *Miss U! Til 2morrow*

I didn't think that much about it. I assumed he'd explain everything when I saw him. But all I got was another text message the next morning: *NO MORE BUS.*

Now I was alarmed. All sorts of things raced through my mind. *No more walks to the bus stop. No more sitting on the bus together. No more meetups after school.*

Then it hit me. *OMG, it's his mother*. She didn't like my dance at the talent show. She probably didn't like my editorial on the dress code. But would she try to rip us apart over such trivial stuff? Worse, was Will siding with his mom?

I needed answers. I sprawled across my bed late that afternoon and sent a brief text to Will: *What's up?*

I watched as he texted back: *Not much*

I sent another text: *LOVE 2 CU L8R*

He texted back: *Busy*

I texted: *When?*

He texted: *?*

Will was ghosting me. I moped in my room over it. Then I plodded into the kitchen where Mom was cooking dinner. I collapsed into a chair and sulked some more.

Finally, I turned toward Mom. "Can we talk?"

"Sure," she said, her back to me as she checked on the chicken in the oven.

"Everyone hates me."

Mom twirled around. "I don't hate you. Gran was right. I came down a little too hard on you at the talent show." She had tweaked her shrill dance review.

I'd also had a change of heart. Yes, it'd dawned

on me that some adults—like my mom—might've been sorta kinda right about some things—like my dance. It struck me in a flash of light that my dance actually might've been too mature for a particular crowd, and that in the future I might want to consider a bigger picture—you know, walk in the shoes of, say, Mrs. Morris before making a big decision that could have a really bad consequence. I mean, I sure never meant to come off as classless to anyone.

"Mom," I said, "I'm really sorry about my dance making people leave the gym."

"I know you are, honey." Then she went over again how I should punch some imaginary Pause button the next time I came up with a cutting-edge idea, consider the aftermath, and maybe check with her. It was pretty much the same stuff she'd blasted me with before but in a lower-key way that was easier to swallow. Plus, it was crazy close to my second thoughts on all of it.

Uh oh, I thought. *Am I becoming my mother?*

She washed some broccoli and placed it in the steamer. "It was mostly Mrs. Morris and her crew making the big fuss."

"Well, the Morrises hate me."

"Oh, they'll come around."

Actually, I only cared about one Morris. "It's Will," I clarified. "He's not talking to me."

Mom turned toward me and crossed her arms. "Give it some time," she advised with a quick bob of her head.

I wandered out of the kitchen and back to my bedroom. I felt better after talking to Mom, but not good enough. The tweenage me wanted to give it some time, but the *almost*-teenage me could not. I slipped out of the house, marched around to Will's bedroom window, and patrolled it. After a while, I picked up some pebbles from the driveway.

What if I break his window? Mrs. Morris will throw a fit. Of course, she already hates me with the heat of the sun and a power that's screwing up my life.

Whatever. I drew back my arm and pitched. Twice. Both stones clipped the wall below the window. The third and fourth hit their mark.

Will's head popped up in the window.

I motioned for him to come down.

He nodded, and a minute later, he was in front of me.

"Hi," he said. Then he just hung out there, not saying anything.

My stomach was full of nervous butterflies. But I stood up straight and hit him with what had been living in my mind rent-free ever since his mom called out Chip for his loose jeans. "You backed up Chip when your mom went after him . . . well, what about me?"

He twisted his face. He rocked back and forth on his feet. He looked down, then away, everywhere except at me.

"Say something," I said almost helplessly.

"What do you want me to say?"

I glared at him. *Really?* I could think of a bunch of things. On the top of the list, would it kill him to pipe up about his mom's crazy plan to ditch the bus?

My chest tightened. I felt heat rising inside of me, and I pushed him on it. "Say something!"

"She's my mom. It's just the two of us."

Crushed, I thought, *What about the two of us?* A lump the size of one of his baseballs was forming in my throat, but I had to say it. "Stand up to your mother . . . for me."

He went mute again, and I got all teary-eyed.

I knew he could see how close I was to losing it, and I thought for sure he would take my side now. Instead, he looked at me with puppy dog eyes and said, "Let's give it some time."

My jaw nearly dropped to the ground. *Worst answer. Ever.* What was he, my mother?

My knight in pirate's clothing lost some of his shine.

I blinked back tears. My resolve crumpled, and I stomped off.

Chapter 25

It was the iconic love scene. He cradled her face gently in his hands. He leaned in and pressed a soft kiss against her cheek. He raised his head slowly, kissing her forehead first, then her eyes, her cheeks. She trembled slightly and bit her lip. He pulled her closer. She relaxed and threw her arms around his neck. They kissed. It was so hot.

Jen and I had found a copy of an old *Twilight* DVD at the library and located a kiss scene that was one of those wow ones, not one or two kisses, but a bunch of them strung together—a total smoochfest. Right now we were so close to my TV set that we were practically inside of it. We were breathing at least as heavily as the characters.

Nothing like my kisses with Will, but still. "What a rush."

"I hear ya," Jen said. "I've got goose bumps."

"I know, I know," I chimed in.

Even we knew how silly we must have sounded. We broke out into hysterical giggles. We were doubled over with the kind of laughing that made your tummy hurt when Mom sailed through the room with some laundry in one hand and a smoothie in the other.

"You girls certainly do entertain each other," she said. Then she glanced down at the DVD cover. "For goodness' sake, how can you be so engrossed in a movie about vampires?"

Jen and I swapped disbelieving looks.

"You wouldn't begin to understand, Mom," I said in my I-know-so-much-more-than-you tone of voice.

"I never cared for vampire stories. I never read the *Twilight* books or saw the movies." She shook her head at us and drifted into the hallway.

We hunkered down for in-depth viewing, dissecting every itty-bitty detail of the kisses. Oddly enough, that was as far as the romance went in this movie. Even so, it was more intense than any kiss we'd ever had, and we did not get bored obsessing over it. Ever.

We zeroed in on a scene where Edward and Bella were alone in the woods. "I think it's really romantic the way Edward takes the lead here," I mentioned.

"I don't know about that," Jen said. "Bella's awfully inviting, gazing up at him with her lips hanging out."

I jabbed her playfully with my elbow. "Come on. They're not exactly pursed into suction cups." I sucked in my cheeks like a fish.

Jen crunched over, laughing. "You're right. But Bella is definitely into him." She straightened up and slipped on her thoughtful face. "What's wrong with the girl getting things going, anyway?"

I shrugged my shoulders. "Nothing."

But isn't the boy supposed to make the first move? Of course, women are leaders in everything else. They're governors of states, CEOs of big companies. Girls, like me, are editors of newspapers. Why not have the girl lead the way in social stuff?

I gave her a friendly nudge. "What about getting something going with Chip? I think you kinda like him."

"*Maaaybe*. But would I kiss him first?" She tipped her head. "I'm just sayin', someone's got to take the first step. I figure the guy's just as scared as I am of feeling stupid if the plan goes south."

"I guess," I said. Then I held up the remote. "One more time?"

She bobbed her head up and down. I hit Play, and we scooted closer to check out the already cued-up Kiss scene again.

"Look at those lips," Jen said, leaning in toward the screen and puckering up her mouth. "Those soft, just slightly parted lips—crying out to you, *Kiss me*."

"Kiss me, kiss me, kiss me," mimicked the unmistakable voice of Max.

Jen and I wheeled around. How long had he been spying on us? My mind raced back to the particulars of our conversation. For a second, we were all caught in a sort of holding pattern. Then the corners of Max's mouth curled up, and he let out a belly laugh before spreading his netted Spider-Man wings in a demo of power and airplane-ing it out of the room.

Jen blushed. "What if Max blabs to Chip about me liking him?" She wrinkled her forehead. "We've gotta shut him up."

"Ha," I snickered. "Short of snuffing him out, what do you propose?"

"I dunno," she said. "Appeal to his better instincts?"

"He doesn't have any."

"Then what?"

We sat there thinking, empty thought bubbles above our heads, until it struck me.

I rubbed my hands together devilishly and grinned. "Trickery!"

Jen brightened. "What's the trick?"

"Oh," I told her in a teasing way, "it's very scientific, proven to work beyond a shadow of a doubt."

"Well, don't keep me in the dark."

I continued the wind up. "You're getting warm. It involves shadows and the dark."

Jen was apparently not in a discovery mood. She threw her hands in the air. "What's all the mystery? Just tell me!"

"Okay, okay." I leaned in and dropped a plan both clever and beautiful. "A total eclipse of the sun," I whispered.

A solar eclipse was coming to Albuquerque, and everyone was making a big deal out of it. A total solar only came around in any one place in hundreds of years, and it was coming here in March.

Jen stared goggle-eyed at me. "Explain." Her voice was flat now, like all of the excitement had been knocked right out of her.

I clarified. "You know, when the moon blocks out the sun."

"That much I do know. Everyone knows," she said with her face full of frown lines.

Actually, she had a good reason for getting impatient. You couldn't go a stone's throw without hearing something about the eclipse. The newspapers and TV stations were full of info about it. It wasn't just the locals getting in on it either. Scientists and a bunch of other eclipse chasers from all over the world were traveling here to plant themselves in the path of its shadow.

Grant Middle was talking it up pretty much nonstop too. The science classes were teaching whole units on eclipses, educating us on how the moon, sun, and Earth had to line up just right for totality to happen. The teachers really harped on how to look at it without burning your eyes to cinders. One DIY way was to poke a hole in a piece of cardboard and look through it at the image projected on the ground. Another much cooler way was to look right up at the sun through specially treated glasses.

The science classes weren't the only ones floodlighting the eclipse. Mr. Garcia even found a way to pull it into one of his English lessons with an excerpt from Mark Twain's novel, *A Connecticut Yankee in King Arthur's Court*. In the story, a regular modern-day mechanic bumped his head and time traveled all the way back to sixth-century England. They were ready to burn him at the stake on account of his weirdness when he leaned on his scientific know-how from the future to predict an eclipse coming that very day to King Arthur's Court. It scared the living daylights out of the Court and saved the mechanic's life. *How dope is that?*

A smile rolled back on Jen's face, and she set off on a rant about some daydream she'd had after Mr. Ramos taught a class on eclipses. "I was walking home," she said all starry-eyed, "when out of the blue Chip popped up, looking smokin' hot as always, and—"

I snapped my fingers to stop her right there.

"Hey! Let's see if we can turn at least one of these fantasies into reality."

Jen pursed her mouth into a tight circle. "Do I have a choice on which one?"

I paused for a sec. I got it. Shutting her down just as she was kicking off her hot dream sequence with Chip was not stellar, especially since she'd listened to me rattle on about Will more than anyone else could stomach.

I fussed at her anyway. "No, you do not have a choice." I set my hands on the sides of my eyes, like blinders. "Focus."

She drummed her fingers on the side of her leg. Finally, the lines around her mouth softened. "Fine," she said.

"Here's the plan," I said. "I'll convince Max that I have the power to turn his day into night if he doesn't keep his motor mouth shut about our TV tea."

"Good one." Her interest piqued. "Do you think you can pull it off?"

I faked a wicked witchy cackle. "Watch me."

We stayed silent for a moment. I slumped down on my bed, and Jen collapsed into my chair. I had come up with a plan on how to deal with my sneaky brother, but I was still fuming about how things stood with Will.

I had options. One, I could forget about Will, which would never happen. Two, I could stage an intervention.

I sighed and broke the silence, sounding off about Will's wimpy response to his mother's scheme to rip us apart. All steamed up, I railed, "Mrs. Morris wants to erase me from the picture! I need to talk to Will. Any ideas?"

"I guess you could tackle him on the field." Jen giggled.

"Funny. That's what he deserves."

We both went quiet for a while, thinking. Then it was like a light bulb switched on in Jen's head. "How about a locker ambush?"

I popped up off the bed and paced the room. Will's locker was all the way on the other side of the building. But he usually dawdled for a while at the end of the day, picking up his sports gear before practice. *If I can corner him in time . . .*

Jen read my mind. "Make it after school. More time to track him down and talk."

"Right. Plus, his mom won't be hovering nearby."

Jen laughed. "Parents can cause so much heartache."

Chapter 26

The next day when the three-thirty dismissal bell rang, I practically raced over to Will's locker. I put on the brakes as I rounded the corner and slowly walked it from there to avoid looking like some sick stalker. I caught him just as he was slamming his locker shut. When he turned around, I was right up in his face.

He took a step back. "Hi, Kat."

"Hey," I said, casually. Then I flipped into girl-boss mode. I stared him right in the eye and squinted. "You've had *some time*. What's the deal?"

He stuffed his hands into his pockets and rocked back and forth on his heels, stalling. Finally, he said, "My mom doesn't want me hanging out with you so much anymore."

I was nervous and a little shaky, but I folded my arms across my chest and pushed him on it. "Obviously," I said. "Why not?"

He peered down the hall at nothing in particular, then back at me. "The truth?"

I nodded my head slowly up and down.

He tried to sugarcoat it. "She doesn't like the way you dance."

I wanted the whole ugly picture. "You mean she thinks I'm classless?"

"Not exactly." He fidgeted with his hands. "But sort of."

"And you?" I asked in a much smaller voice.

He pumped his hand over his heart. "Me? I love your dancing."

Suddenly, my whole world filled with sunshine. I uncrossed my arms and grinned one of those big-toothed grins. It felt like the universe revolved around just the two of us, and no one—not even Mrs. Morris—could slide in between and muck things up. Then Will leaned in and kissed me, and I walked on air.

"I miss the school bus," Will said.

"I miss you on the bus," I said.

We beamed sappy, happy faces back and forth at each other and giggled for a ridiculously long time.

Then Will stepped back and explained that his mom could be difficult. *Like I didn't know that.*

He said he went along with her, thinking that the whole thing would blow over soon, or that she'd just get tired of driving him to school. Then he smacked his forehead, admitted he'd read her all wrong, and apologized all over the place.

"My bad. So sorry, Kat. *So very, very sorry.*" He went on and on like that.

I slouched back against the lockers. I nodded. Finally, I held up my hand. "Okay. Enough. Stop."

It wasn't all his fault. He hadn't danced the dance or written the editorial that set off his mom. Even more than that, he hadn't built himself up to be some shining knight from the world of make-believe. I had. Funny thing, I didn't long for a prince or a pirate from Fantasyland anymore. I ached for a real live boy with all of his hang-ups included. What if Will wasn't perfect? Neither was I. *We all know that.*

I rolled away from the lockers. "Now," I said in a totally no-nonsense, down-to-earth girl sort of way, "what can we do about this?"

I didn't have a problem sneaking around behind Mrs. Morris's back, but Will did. Anyway, Mrs. M. and her friends' prying eyes were everywhere, so she'd probably find out. An outright lie wouldn't work. We needed some likely story that she could buy into, a little fib to spare her feelings and get us back together at the same time.

Will came up with a doozy. "How about an eclipse date?"

I loved the idea. "Sneaky," I said. "I approve." But I was already having second thoughts about how it'd actually work. I sighed. "Why would your mom let us go together?"

"Because I'll tell her there is no way I can cancel on such a big *preplanned* date." He winked at me.

I winked back.

Both of our heads wagged with pleasure.

Our date was on. Will trotted off to his baseball practice, and I skipped halfway down the hall on the way to my *Grantline* meeting.

———————

Word of the eclipse had gone out in the newspaper quite a while ago, and the science classes had been talking it up nonstop. But our March newsletter was scheduled to come out right before the eclipse. It was our job to update the story.

Our whole staff of eight got in on it. I oversaw

assignments on all the stories. Of course, Ms. Ramirez had the last say on them.

Here was the story lineup:

Special glasses and their distribution centers. (Story and photo). *Check*.

Free bus pickup listings. *Check*.

Best locations for viewing. Multiple articles. (On-site visits and photos). *Check*.

Best food and music venues. *Check*.

It took tons of work and loads of nagging to make the deadline. We were still churning out rewrites on sub-standard stories and concocting catchy headlines for them on the printer's due date. Ms. Ramirez planted herself at her computer with me at her side. The rest of the staffers, coached and hurried on by our lead news writer, Ruby, dashed back and forth with their revised copy. I handled the last edits. Ms. Ramirez did the final signoffs.

We were down to the wire, but we did it— we fit all the final bits and pieces of the paper together. I had the honor of pressing the button on the computer, sending our special issue off for publication.

With interest at its peak just two days before

the event, we distributed our full newsletter with an up-to-date collection of articles and photos on everything you could possibly want to know about the eclipse. To maximize sales, two of us positioned ourselves in the cafeteria and two in the main lobby. The rest of us marched in and out of classrooms and all around campus.

Usually, we had to hawk the paper to homeroom classes the next morning, and we'd still have some left over. This time kids were dropping by the office asking for copies. By late afternoon, we were forced to post a Sold Out sign on the *Grantline* door. It was our most widely circulated issue. Ever.

"Kudos to the *Grantline Newsletter* staff for a job well done on the eclipse," blared Principal Gray's voice over the PA system during morning announcements the next day. "And a special shout-out to the editor, Kat Cruz, and our club sponsor, Ms. Ramirez."

In homeroom, everyone's eyes fixed on me—everyone's—and in the best possible way this time. One student clapped, and some others joined in. I snuck a quick peek at Maria. She gave me a single, very slow clap. Not much, but a lot for Maria.

I glowed like a shining star. My heart was full and my smile was broad. Even when I narrowed the smile, so as not to appear too full of myself, I could not keep the edges of my mouth from popping up. You would have thought I'd won the Journalist of the Year Award. That was how good I felt.

At the end of the day, Principal Gray was back on the loudspeaker once more with a final pep talk for all Grant Middle School students.

"No excuses now," he bellowed. "Everyone, go out and see the eclipse!"

Chapter 27

A total solar eclipse would be visible in Albuquerque today. The time was ripe for action.

It was a beautiful morning in March, and the birds were chirping when I moseyed out to the backyard. Max was hanging out in a polo shirt and khaki cargos on Dad's miniature golf course. He'd been putting away for a while at hole one.

"Want to play?" he asked.

"No thanks. I'll just watch."

After a few more missed shots, I set my scheme in motion.

"Remember when you said you thought you had superpowers?" I asked, my voice all easy-breezy.

Max turned to face me. He folded his arms. "I do have superpowers."

The polo shirt had replaced the Superman tee, but Max's comeback was solid superhero, which was what I counted on.

I rolled my eyes. "Are you faster than a speeding bullet?"

"No."

"Can you leap tall buildings in a single bound?"

"No."

"Then you are not Superman."

"I didn't say I was *the* Superman. I said I was *a* superman." He smiled smugly.

Playing along, I told him that I guessed this superpower thing ran in the family because I had some special powers too. He just shrugged and turned back to his golfing, as if he thought his silly claims were all true-blue but mine were a big bunch of baloney.

I sighed. But I didn't let it throw me. "Okay, Mr. Smarty Pants. Here's the deal. If I don't like what you do, I'll turn your whole world dark."

Max twirled around and leaned over his golf club like he was some smooth tournament player. He jutted out his chin and screwed up his face. "I don't believe you."

"You don't believe me, Mr. Golf, because I've never used my power on you. I figured you were just a little kid, and I let you slide." I got right up in his face. "Well, you're not a baby anymore, and if you cross me or Jen by dropping even the smallest detail from one of our private talks—say, the one about kissing—I will use my superpowers to blot the light of day out of your life."

I was hoping for him to be scared. The last thing I expected was crowing. "You're right. I'm no baby. I'm in second grade." He dumped his golf club, snatched up a piece of cardboard from a lawn chair, and stabbed his finger at a hole in the middle of it. "Pinhole viewer," he explained, giggling his head off.

Second graders know about eclipses? Okay, so Max knew he couldn't look directly at the sun, but the half-pint know-it-all didn't know everything.

I switched gears and went with what I had left. "Good for you," I said. "Little kids make pinhole viewers and see puny reflections on the ground." I whipped out my special glasses and put them on. "Big kids have custom-made eclipse glasses. I can stare right up at the sun with these. Pretty cool, huh?" I took the glasses off and waved them around in front of him.

He grabbed for them. "Let me see."

"Not so fast." I held them high. "I need to wear them when all the *cool* kids go outside to watch the eclipse."

"I want some," he whined.

"Of course you do," I said. And that was when I cast my final hook and reeled him in. I told him that I could *possibly* loan him an extra pair of the special glasses I had, but that he would have to give me something in return.

"Like what?" He stuck out his lower lip in a full pout.

I pushed my face right up in his. "Like your promise to keep your mouth shut about my conversation with Jen in front of the TV the other day."

He cocked his head to the side, thinking it over.

Did I mention that dealing with Max was never a slam dunk? He didn't give up anything easily. But neither did I. I drummed my fingers on one of the yard chairs. Fed up with waiting for him, I made the savvy decision to walk.

Max caved. "Hold up," he called. "I promise."

"Okay then," I said and handed him the specs. *Mission accomplished.*

He grinned, looked at those glasses every

which way, and grinned some more. Then, with big eyes, he asked, "When should I put them on?"

"Uh . . ."

I wasn't sure what to tell him. I had a not-to-be-missed eclipse date with Will. As usual, Mom and Dad were working at the gym. The plan was to drop off Max there, where he probably wouldn't see anything.

"Um," I said again.

He seemed so genuinely excited about seeing the eclipse, especially after I'd set him up for it by dangling my cool glasses in front of him. I felt kinda guilty about the big buildup to the letdown coming around the corner.

"Don't worry," I said, mussing his hair. "I'll let you know about the glasses."

Okay, so I felt bad for him, and a touch of a sisterly feeling crept in. I didn't have to, but I decided to bring him along. Anyway, I was getting too old to get any real kick out of tricking a little kid, even if he was my pain-in-the-neck brother.

We knew the number-one place to go for the best viewing of this rare total solar eclipse because of the *Grantline*'s ace reporting. We knew about the music, the food, pretty much everything. So later that day, Will, Max, and I squeezed onto one of the packed shuttle buses at the mall and headed for the rec center. We streamed onto the recreation fields with hundreds of other people, maybe thousands. It was like an early Fourth of July. There were Jumbotrons set up, plus some local bands and a bunch of food stands. We bought some tacos and sodas and scoped out a good spot for the show.

"Look," Max said, pointing wide-eyed at the broad-brimmed hats and silver-studded outfits of a mariachi band. We spread our blanket and sat down next to the mariachis, ate, and listened to their songs of love and betrayal. And we waited.

Max was getting restless after a while. "Nothing's happening," he complained. "Think it's a dud?" he asked, as if it were some firecrackers that hadn't gone off.

"Hold your horses, little dude," Will said. "This show is guaranteed to come off."

"How do you know?"

"Force of nature," he explained.

Max shrugged and looked up. "When?"

Will winked at me and pulled out a pack of cards from his pocket. "Let's play War."

Max was so absorbed by his winning streak that he didn't even notice at first that something extraordinary was going on. The sky was growing darker. It looked like a gigantic filter was sliding slowly over the sun. We stood up and put on our solar eclipse glasses. Will held my hand. Max grabbed my other hand. Together our human chain link gazed skyward. The dark shadow of the moon slowly blocked out the bright light of the sun's face. We couldn't look away.

"Unreal," Max said. "I don't even think Superman could do this."

I stared down at him, realizing that it was pretty special that a kid his age was even interested in an eclipse.

"Force of nature," Will said.

I peeked over at him. It was really great how good he was with Max. I squeezed both of their hands.

Together we saw the sun's crescents, and finally the ring of fire with sparks of light shooting out all around the moon, like some sort of otherworldly fireworks, as it covered almost all of the sun. It was spectacular.

I snuck a second glance at Will. *He's spectacular too.*

Chapter 28

The next day, Jen and I were set to take in another viewing of *Twilight* when my mom paraded through the room.

"Mom," I said. "Can't we have any privacy?"

"It's a family room shared by all, I'm afraid." She glanced over at the TV. "Not that vampire thing again."

I tried to plug her into reality. "What you don't realize, Mom," I said, dropping my chin and raising both eyebrows for a meaningful look, "is that this is an iconic film."

She still had no clue. "That drivel." She playfully drew her face back into her neck. "I'm not so sure about that."

"Well, there is one thing I am sure about," I said, gushing with certainty. "The kiss scene is amazing."

"Ha," pooh-poohed Mom. She pulled out one of Gran's old videos and soft-shoed it over to me.

"If a good kissing scene is what you're after, try this one."

The *Some Like It Hot* jacket was faded and worn. "Is it from the Stone Age?" I asked.

"Noooo," droned Mom, popping it into Gran's old tape machine and fast-forwarding. To check the scene, she hit Play.

"Oh no!" I squealed. "It's in black and white."

Jen and I carried out simultaneous jaw drops. Mom hit Fast Forward again.

"Oh my God." I was gaping open-mouthed at the VHS tape jacket. "Look, Jen. It's from 1959."

"Wow," she said. "Is it a silent movie?"

We were having a good laugh when Mom stopped the tape at a really funny scene when Marilyn Monroe was throwing her arms around some nerdy guy with glasses. We couldn't help but stop and look. For a minute we were transfixed. And that brought me to a sort of standstill and made me think that maybe my mom wasn't as clueless as I thought.

Mom hit Pause. "I'll leave you two modern-day snobs with this notion: some lessons can be learned from things older than last week."

When she was gone, I wanted to hit Play to continue with the scene, but Jen gripped my arm.

Deep lines creased her forehead. "Something's happened . . . something big . . . and I need to talk."

I didn't know what could be bigger than a good kissing scene, but she seemed really pressed about it.

"Yesterday." She twisted her whole face as she struggled to find the words. "It happened really fast."

"What happened really fast? I'm not following."

"Chip."

"Go on." I twirled my finger in a circle, encouraging her.

She told me that Chip had called her at the last minute, and they'd ended up watching the eclipse together from the roof of his apartment building.

She lowered her voice to a whisper. "We kissed when the lights went out."

"OMG!" I leaned in. "Tell me everything. In detail."

She grinned. "I made the first move and kissed him."

"Way to go, Jen!"

"But it was only one of those small kisses."

Suddenly, just when her story was picking up steam, she ended it.

Naturally, I was high-key invested. "Congrats," I said. "And?"

Jen smiled weakly. She slouched over, locked her arms across her chest, and slowed the pace of her storytelling way down. "It was awkward . . . I thought he was trying to slip his arm around my back to pull me closer . . . but his hand landed on my boob." Her voice wobbled a little bit, and she hesitated.

Of course, I was dying to hear what happened next. So I pushed her very gently on it. "Keep going," I said in a super-soft voice.

She gave me a look. Then she fastened her arms even tighter around her body, pinning her hands to her shoulders like in a straitjacket. "I pushed his hand away. He put it back. I told him to stop. He didn't, and I yelled *NO* kinda loud." She bit her lip, and her words grew more hesitant and heavier. "It was getting lighter, and people turned to look at us." She blinked back tears.

I could feel her heartache. "That's messed up," I said. "He was way out of line. And you absolutely did the right thing by telling him to stop." I rested my hand on her shoulder and squeezed.

She crunched over and let her head sink into her hands.

I wanted to be supportive and cheer her up. But when she lifted her head, I saw that her cheeks were wet and her eyes were swollen. So, I just wrapped my arm around her and hugged her.

Jen and I were hanging outside the PE classes when my nemesis Maria came marching toward us with her laser-look riveted on me.

Oh no, I thought. *What is it this time? What can she possibly have on me?*

Totally unexpected, she shifted her gaze to Jen. She reached out her arm and plopped down her hand on Jen's shoulder.

Jen flinched.

"Stand strong," Maria said. "Girl power."

Jen tilted her head.

"Chip," Maria said. "He's a loser."

We both tilted our heads.

Maria smiled coyly. "I have my sources."

Jen looked at her with a questioning eye.

"Boys like Chip need to keep their wandering hands to themselves," Maria said. "Full stop. Period."

Just then, Chip strode by on his way to PE. Maria tapped him as he passed. He turned to face her. She narrowed her eyes at him, took two fingers and pointed them at her eyes, and then at his. "Watch it. I've got my eyes on you," she said nastily.

Chip flipped a dismissive hand at her, shot her one of his famous smirks, and strutted off with attitude. Still, even he had to know that getting on Maria's sour side was a scary thing.

"Later, loser!" Maria called after him.

Maria, Jen, and I all wore full-toothed grins.

Imagine, an alliance with Maria.

Chapter 29

A bunch of the seniors at Gran's Sunrise House piled into the TV room every Monday night to watch *Dancing with the Stars,* to take in the dances and call in their votes. A group of them got it in their heads that, with lessons, they could become just like the celebrity contestants. Gran, the only dancer in the lot, led the push to bring ballroom to Sunrise. She nagged the program director until she hired an instructor.

On April first, the Sunrise dancers had their first class, but the lesson did not go well. According to the program lady that Mom had spoken with, Gran disagreed with the teacher over the proper way to perform the Argentine tango. But when Gran was asked to demonstrate, she couldn't remember a single step.

Gran had stormed off in a huff and locked herself in her room. The Sunrise lady called Mom to come over and help get Gran settled down. In turn, Mom told me she had an emergency. She said she had to visit Gran right away. Dad was at the gym and I was home, so she said she was putting her "grown-up daughter" in charge of Max.

Really? Suddenly, I was a grown-up just when I didn't want to be.

She tossed in that she saw no need for us to stay in all day. "You can take Max with you to the mall. It will be fun."

I cringed. "Fun for who?"

She rattled on about how I could stop at the toy store while I was there and check out what kind of balls and bats Max might like for his birthday. She smiled at Max, who was playing with his marbles on the living room floor. "Dad wants to get him ready for Little League tryouts next month."

More fun.

I took as fair-minded an approach as I could and explained to her politely that I already had plans to meet up at the mall with Jen and a couple of other friends from the *Grantline* for a movie, one that was not for little kids. "As you can see," I said reasonably enough, "toting Max along will ruin everything."

"Kat," she said, crossing her arms. "Sometimes plans have to change."

"And sometimes they don't," I said. "Why can't you hire a babysitter?"

Mom let out a loud sigh. Then she calmly explained to me that dragging an antsy Max with her to the Sunrise House, where she would have to put her full focus on Gran, would be nearly impossible, and that it was just too late to line up a babysitter. "This is last minute," she said. "Gran needs me now, and I need you."

Yes, I was grown-up enough to know an emergency when it was staring me in the face. "Fine," I said. "But I promise you, I'm not going to have any fun."

We lived close to the mall, and the plan was to walk. Well, I walked and Max skateboarded. Dad had given him the board for his seventh birthday. He would stand on it, sit on it, lie on it, and sometimes ram me with it. I didn't want him bringing the thing, but Mom thought it would be okay.

"It'll keep him focused on the journey," she assured me.

So Max packed the board under his arm and headed for the door. On his way out, he grabbed a handful of marbles that were scattered on the living room floor and jammed them into his pocket.

"Mooooom?" I said. "You know they could turn into missiles."

"Kat, he'll be fine," she said.

Despite the potential for disaster, everything seemed to be going smoothly. Then just before we got to the mall, Max decided he was really thirsty. He whined and whined until we stopped at the 7-Eleven. He wanted a Slurpee, his favorite treat.

Outside the store, one, then another, and another of Max's precious marbles started falling through a hole in his pocket. One rolled under my foot and I seesawed.

"All of your marbles for a Slurpee," I called out to prevent a full-blown danger zone.

Max giggled and turned them over.

I stuffed the marbles into my pocket. Max tucked his skateboard under his arm and bolted through the door. He headed straight for the Slurpee machine.

A couple of cute boys wearing high school

letterman jackets walked in with me. One held the door open. "Thanks," I said. I watched the two of them as they headed toward the cooler at the back of the store.

A ratty-looking guy tramped in behind me and bumped my shoulder as he brushed by. We glanced at each other for a sec. He had greasy ringlets of hair and a stubbly chin. A gaping hole in his jeans made it look like they were falling off, and his T-shirt was food-stained, as if he'd used it for a tablecloth at his last meal. He scowled and moved on.

I scanned the store to check on Max. I spotted him standing in line to get a Slurpee.

Right then, the scruffy guy who had knocked into me pushed right up to the front of the checkout line.

"Hey, I'm next," squawked a gray-haired man who was standing at the counter. He fished dollar bills out of his wallet. He was about to hand them to the cashier when everything went berserk.

"I say I'm next." The ratty-looking guy pulled out a gun and ordered everyone to get back. He told the young cashier to fork over all the money in the register. Then he turned to the gray-haired man. "And I'll take those dollar bills, too, old man." Smirking, he held out his hand. Shaking, the man placed his money gingerly in the thief's palm.

"*Dios salve la situación*," chanted a woman near me. She crossed herself and gazed upward.

Those of us on the fringes morphed into statues. The customers near the counter, including Max, followed the thief's orders and shrank away.

All I wanted to do was race over to Max and hold him close, but I was frozen by fear. I stood there with everyone and watched the cashier shovel money into a paper bag. When he dropped some of the money, he apologized all over the place. "So sorry, so clumsy, so sorry."

"Hurry it up," ordered the thief. His voice sent shivers through me.

With no resistance, the robber snatched up the bag full of money, did a one-eighty, and was all set to make his getaway when Max kicked his skateboard hard and rammed it into the thief's shins. My mouth hung open in shock. *What was he thinking?* No way could Max's superhero antics save him from this grown man.

"Ouch!" shrieked the thief. "What do you think you're doin'?" He reached down to shove the board away from his legs. "Dang kids," he growled.

Max and I looked at each other. *The neighborhood burglar without the mask?*

Max edged a couple of steps back.

I stared in horror as the scum-bum righted himself and started for Max. "You little punk," he roared.

"Max!" I shouted. I had to do something to protect my little brother. Quickly, I grabbed a bunch of magazines and heaved them at the loser. "He's a kid! Leave him alone!" I cried. My heart pounded as adrenaline coursed through my veins, and I barreled toward them.

The thief tossed Max aside against the counter and smacked me hard on the side of my face with the back of his hand. Pain exploded in my eye. I flew backward into the magazine rack, bashing my head on the metal corner. Blood trickled down my shirt. My head throbbed.

Suddenly, the two high schoolers jumped in to help.

"I've got this," one of the boys called out. He grabbed the thief's arm and twisted it behind his back. But the thief turned and punched him hard in the gut with his free fist, sending him reeling.

"You're going down," the other boy muttered under his breath. He came at him from behind, clasping him around the chest, but the thief delivered a high-impact elbow to his ribs, breaking his hold. Then he made for the door.

Don't let him get away, I thought. Max's skateboard was within reach, so I grabbed it and thrust it forward with all my might to trip him up. It slammed into the back of his legs. He stumbled.

By the time he regained his balance, I whipped out one final battle trick stuffed in my pocket—a handful of marbles. I rolled the marbles fast under the thief's feet. First, he fish-tailed. Then, his feet flew out from under him, and he dive-bombed to the ground with a terrible thump. He rallied briefly, climbing to his feet on wobbly legs.

"Take this!" cried one of the high school boys, whacking him over the head with his soda bottle.

The thief scrunched over on bent knees.

Then both of the high schoolers pounced on top of him and held him there while the clerk called the police.

Meanwhile, I ran to Max, and Max tried to run to me, but he had banged his head on the counter and twisted his wrist when he fell. I thought he might shake it off Superman-style and bounce right up. Instead, he slumped back down against the counter and lay there with the wind knocked out of him. I slipped down beside him, and we stayed there, holding on to each other until help came.

When the police showed up, everyone was talking at once, so it took a while to get the details straight. As the story was unraveling, an ambulance pulled up. The driver got out and talked to Max and me.

"Are you okay? Are you okay?"

"Not so good," I said.

"Hurts," Max mumbled.

The two emergency guys packed us up in their ambulance and whisked us over to the hospital.

Chapter 30

Things slowed way down in the emergency room. The ambulance guys checked us in, shifted us onto hospital beds, and left. A nurse pulled a circular curtain around us, then forgot about us.

The next thing I knew, Mom was there, sounding slightly hysterical on the other side of the curtain. "Oh my God! Oh my God!" she kept saying.

"They're going to be fine," the nurse kept reassuring her.

Mom was just sniffling a little when the nurse pulled the curtain aside.

Sad to say, Mom's jaw nearly dropped to the floor when she saw our swollen heads, and she got emotional all over again. "Oh, my babies, my poor babies," she whimpered. "Are you okay?"

"Nooooo," Max and I moaned in unison.

Mom blinked back tears. "Why'd you do it?" she whispered with her mouth all shaky.

"No one else was doing anything," Max said.

Mom pinched her eyebrows together. "Max. You should never fight a man who is trying to rob a store. Ever." When her little Superman wannabe didn't answer, she shifted her attention to me. "You should've known better."

"Me?" I protested. "I barely moved a muscle until the guy went after Max."

"Well, why couldn't someone older have leaped in to save the day?" she blustered. She carried on like that and kept us company while Dad took care of some paperwork. The hospital had been waiting for my parents to give them health information and sign insurance forms.

Just then, Dad slipped through the curtain with the doctor to check us out.

"I hear we have some heroes in here," the doctor said.

"And some reporters sticking around outside for interviews." Dad smiled. He moved between our beds and squeezed my hand and Max's shoulder. "Looks like no one puts down my little superman or messes with my grown-up daughter without paying a price for it," he said cheerily.

Then he pinned his eyes just on me, and his voice got all serious and a little gushy. "I'm so proud of you," he said, "for stepping up at that crucial moment to shield your brother from what could have been a catastrophic attack." He kept looking at me, like he really wanted his words of thanks to sink in.

Max interrupted. "My head hurts," he complained.

"Well then. Let's have a look at the damages," the doctor said. He checked the big bump on Max's head first. He pressed lightly on it.

Max winced.

The doctor poked and prodded the rest of his skull without much reaction. Then he examined Max's floppy wrist. He lifted it gently.

"Ouch," Max groaned, pulling it away.

Next, the doctor turned his focus on me. "Looks like you got a little roughed up taking care of your brother." He cupped my chin with his hand and rotated my head to get the full picture. "That eye is turning into some shiner," he said. Then he inspected the jagged cut on my head. "I think we're going to need stitches to close this up."

The doctor ordered X-rays and whatnot for both of us. Then we were whooshed over to the lab where a perky nurse announced, "Test time." It took like forever before we were back where we'd started in the ER consulting with the doctor again.

"Luckily," he said, "no permanent injuries." He told us that Max had fractured his wrist and would have to wear a cast for a while. About our heads, he said they were hard—no signs of any concussions. He told me that the stitches in my head would dissolve, and my black eye, which would likely turn every shade of red, black, blue, and finally yellow, would eventually fade.

Prescriptions were written, appointments were scheduled, and we were finally ready to leave. But even then, the doctor stopped us. "Aren't you forgetting something?" he asked Max.

Max tilted his head. "Huh?"

"That cast you're wearing is a badge of courage," he explained. "You're going to have to let your friends have a piece of it by putting their John Hancocks on it."

Max wrinkled his nose. "What's a John Hancock?"

"It's a signature, proof that someone is part of a heroic show of bravery." With that, the doctor initialed the cast while Max giggled and everyone else hanging around in the ER grinned.

As things stood when we rolled out of the hospital, I had a head half shaved with three stitches in it and a bruised eye three times the size of my other one. Max had a Band-Aid on his forehead and a small cast on his wrist.

Max played up that cast pretty big, waving it in front of the cameras and raising it high in the air in a show of triumph. I cringed at being photographed in such horrible shape. With my head shaved on the right side and my eye a swollen red mess on the left, I was in no mood to be interviewed.

The local TV station had sent a news crew to cover the story. When I veered away, the reporter questioned Max first.

"How did you feel about stopping the robbery?" she asked.

"Good," he said.

"And?" She seemed to be after something more spun out, but he wasn't breathing another word. So she tried a more rousing question to tug it out of him. "How about when the bad guy walked up to the front of the line and demanded the money?"

That did get a rise out of Max. He planted his hands on his hips and puffed out the big letter *S* on his little chest. "I got mad. My Gran taught me that the first to come should be the first to get served, and I was there first with my Slurpee."

"You weren't afraid at all?" She kept bobbing her head up and down, encouraging him to add some steamy details.

Instead, he blew cool and clammed up.

I guess she thought she might get more out of me. She turned and jabbed the microphone under my chin.

I shoved it away.

The reporter sighed and lowered the mic. "You know, Max isn't the only hero here."

We reached a compromise. The video of me would be of my left side only, and I would wear a stylish patch over my bruised eye. Adjustments were made and the mic was back in my face.

"Kat," said the reporter. "Would you say you and your brother are natural-born action heroes?"

I did a double take. "I'd say that's a stretch. But we are an athletic family. Our parents own a gym."

Mom and Dad loved this part. Huge smiles stretched across their faces. I knew how reporting worked. Someone would take a picture or video of the outside of our gym and splash it on the screen when the story was aired. Then maybe more people would be drawn to sign up for Cruz's Athletic Club. *Yay!*

"But, Kat," said the reporter back on topic, "don't you think that your behavior and your brother's was extraordinary? I mean the way you both flew into action at that 7-Eleven." She said it in all seriousness and with a sort of hero worship usually saved for bigger-than-life superheroes in the movies.

Clearly, Max and I did not have any super-powers. As a matter of fact, for most of my life, I'd thought my brother's behavior was beyond annoying. But maybe he wasn't just an ordinary kid. I figured what he had were super skills—*real life magic*—that he'd been fine-tuning forever and was not shy about using.

"Frankly," I said, "I'm not that surprised about my brother. He's a little superman."

The reporter smiled. "And what about you? The way you charged at the robber like some superhuman wrecking ball was incredible."

"Well," I crowed, laying it on pretty thick, "when lives are at stake, you act."

The reporter circled both of her hands like

miniature windmills, motioning for me to add more.

"You know that he went after my kid brother. No way could I let that slide. Mostly, I just wanted to protect my brother."

The human side of the story—maybe more than the supernormal—seemed to broaden the reporter's smile all the way across her face.

Then the police came by with a local newspaper reporter trailing behind them. The police checked with the doctor about our injuries and double-checked with us on a lot of info they'd heard at the crime scene. We answered loads of questions.

Then the *Albuquerque Journal* reporter stepped up, hungry for the kids' angle to the story.

Max puffed out his chest with the big Superman logo on it, and the reporter snapped a photo.

"I understand you risked your life to take down the thief at the 7-Eleven," the reporter said.

"Yes, sir," Max said. "It's what any superman would do."

The reporter smiled and turned to me.

I immediately stretched out my arm, palm up. "No photo, please."

He agreed, and I was more than willing to go on the record.

I gave the *Journal* reporter the exclusive on our story with a blow-by-blow on the part that skateboard, magazines, and marbles played in the takedown. I backtracked and told him about how we'd first crossed paths with the burglar on Halloween. And I mentioned the article I'd written for the *Grantline Newsletter* where I alerted middle schoolers about the robber terrorizing our neighborhood.

The reporter told me that the *Albuquerque Journal* was starting a "Tales Out of School" column with a group of contributing student writers. He said he thought I would be perfect for the job.

I almost collapsed with happiness. That was how spesh that was.

The next day, the *Journal* ran the story of the robbery with a sidebar on Max and me—who became the town's heroes overnight. It was a big *W* any way you looked at it.

Chapter 31

T his story got better. The police came around the next day to ask some more questions and gave us an update on the investigation. They told us the 7-Eleven robber was one and the same as the Crystal Park thief. Of course, Max and I already knew that. They said they had recovered a whole lot of stolen property from his apartment, including some of Lily Morris's stuff.

At first, we didn't know what to think when Mrs. Morris came knocking at our door.

"I knew we'd catch that despicable thief if we kept our eyes peeled for him," she said with a ginormous smile, even though she had nothing to do with his capture.

We all stared at her in blank astonishment.

Before any of us could say anything about it, Mrs. Morris yammered on. "I hope all of you will be the honored guests tomorrow at my victory celebration for the neighbors on the block and a few of my close personal friends."

"Of course," Dad said, always out to create goodwill among the neighbors. "Our privilege."

"Oh, and you can invite some of Kat's and Max's school friends," she added as an afterthought.

"Love to," Mom said, thrilled to be back in Mrs. Morris's good graces.

"Splendid," Mrs. Morris said, chummy as if they were besties. She turned to leave, then swiveled back around. "I can't wait to get back to the gym." She winked at us.

OMG! I bit my lip to keep from saying anything.

Mrs. Morris didn't just rejoin Cruz's Athletic Club, she brought her whole gang of Crystal Park women friends back with her, plus some new friends she'd met at Silver's Gym. Seemed they didn't have anything like Dance Party or Just Dance there. *Yay for the Cruzes!* She wasn't about to miss anyone either. She asked us for more enrollment forms to pass out at the party. Mom and Dad were on cloud nine.

Maybe Mrs. M. wasn't so bad now that she was on our side.

———

The next day, my whole family got a rousing round of applause when we showed up at Mrs. Morris's yard party. Some of our neighbors were hungry for the inside scoop on the robbery. Others just wanted to be around us. Maria, who was the daughter of one of Mrs. M.'s close friends, even gave me a nod, like maybe she was hoping my new popularity would rub off on her.

"I'll get my mom to sign up for your gym," she babbled as if she were doing me some humongous favor. "Then we can do that Dance Party class together."

"You mean the classless one?" I asked.

Her mouth clamped shut. *Small blessings.* Then she danced around it. "Well . . . um . . . I'm willing to try it."

I turned my back on her and walked away. But I dragged my feet and slowed my steps. This revenge-is-sweet wasn't really working for me anymore. And what about our girls' alliance?

I turned and waved her toward me, and she scrambled over.

"Maybe we can try a Just Dance class together."

She grinned. "Yes!"

Talk about a 360-degree turnaround. Mind-boggling.

"Okay, then," I said. "See you at the gym."

I walked away with a spring in my step this time. "Bring Luce," I hollered over my shoulder at her before melting into the crowd.

I headed straight for Jen, my constant confidant and adviser.

"Seen Will?" I asked.

"Nope."

"Maybe he's with Chip."

Jen rolled her eyes. "Chip is a loser. I told him off the other day. See that guy over there? James. I've kind of got my eye on him." She waggled her finger and pointed at one of the semi-heroic high schoolers from the 7-Eleven.

"Oh," I said, surprised. "Since when?"

"Since right now."

We both giggled.

"I'm fixed on Will." I sighed and confessed that he'd mostly been keeping it on the down-low again since the eclipse. Still, I told her that I'd gotten an extra sweet text from him earlier that day. I blushed. "It said, 'You're my hero.'"

"Impressive," Jen said. Then she gave me my

marching orders. "You're the 'It' girl right now. Take advantage of it. Confront him."

"You're right," I said with a nod that left my nose pointing straight up in the air. "I'm so famous, he's lucky I'll even talk to him."

She gave me a friendly jab in the shoulder. "You go, girl." Then she was off to meet James.

Armed with my new heroic rep, I moved through the crowd in the yard and entered the kitchen where large sandwich and dessert trays were set up on an enormous marble island. A bunch of parents were standing there chatting, but no Will. Then I meandered into the dining room where a white cloth-covered table was packed with drinks and snacks. A crystal chandelier hung above it. Will's house was much fancier than ours.

I tracked down Will there. "I need answers," I demanded without even blinking.

This time he was quick to explain how his mother had doubled down on him after the eclipse, monitoring everything. "She's been on my case nonstop about even talking to you."

My mind wandered to a bad place. *Oh no. Second thoughts? Siding with his mom?*

Will's voice pulled me back into the conversation. "That's all changed," he was saying.

"Oh." I paused. "What's changed?"

He told me that he and his mom had finally had it out about my dancing and agreed that it was actually not anything worth getting too excited about.

I gaped at him, shocked that things were breaking my way. "You stood up for me?" I asked in a tiny voice.

"Uh-huh." A big toothy grin spread across his face. "Long time coming, but I'm back on the bus."

It took a minute for me to catch up and assess. Then my heart soared like a phoenix rising from the ashes. People were all around us, but I couldn't help it. I locked my arms around him and pulled him into a hug. When I loosened my hold, my eyes were all watery and I think his were a little bit too.

And just like that, we were back on track.

———

I wasn't the only one scoring kudos for our heroics. All of Max's friends at Mrs. M.'s party had a go at scrawling their initials on his cast. Of course, Max had been careful to save a special space for one particular girl: Sue, a seven-year-old cutie in his second-grade class. When Sue signed, she made quite a big show of it, using swirling letters with curlicues. But nothing stood out more than the heart she drew all the way around it. Max kept looking at that heart and touched it for a long time afterward when he thought no one could see. He couldn't seem to stop.

At the end of the day, just as the party was breaking up, Sue ran over to Max and stood right in front of him. She looked very serious. She definitely had something on her mind.

"What?" Max asked.

Sue didn't say anything. She just leaned forward and gave him a peck on the cheek. Then she ran to her mother and buried her face in the folds of her skirt. "Bye," she said from inside the skirt as she and her mom left.

Max touched his hand softly to his cheek. Her kiss was a special gift, and he treasured it, maybe even more than being a hero.

I bent down and whispered in his ear, "Max and Sue sittin' in a tree."

He giggled.

"Hey, kiddo, what if I say that at your next party?"

His eyes snapped wide open. "N-n-no," he said, tripping all over the word.

"What are you going to do to stop me?" I knew I had him in a corner.

He knew it, too, and for the first time, I think he got it. "I promise," he swore, crossing his heart with his finger. "I will never do it to you again if you swear off doing it to me."

"Oh, I don't know." I hesitated, looked away, sighed, and screwed up my face like I was thinking really hard about it—the way he always did.

"Please, Kattie. I'm double sorry. Triple please."

"Oh, okay," I said. "I'm not really into these childish games anymore. You can stop your sloppy begging. We've got a deal."

Max squinched up his face, I guess still not sure about how rock-solid our deal was. "Should we maybe sign something in blood?" he asked.

"No, silly." I laughed. "That's disgusting. I think a pinkie swear ought to do it."

So a pinkie swear was what we did.

Chapter 32

Jen came to chew over an urgent matter that I'd texted her about earlier. "Something life-changing is about to happen."

We were huddled together in my room, and I said it again, "A milestone is about to be crossed." I shot her one of my I-know-you-know-what-I'm-talking-about side glances and flashed her a coy, pursed-lipped smile.

She scrunched her face and placed her hand under her chin in the *Thinker* position. "May Day," she finally blundered out.

Yes, it was May first, announcing the birth of a new month and another *major* birthday coming up. "Try again," I said.

"Umm." She squished her eyes shut, like she was concentrating really hard. She opened them. "Honest to God, I'm clueless."

"You must be joking," I said with a seriously wounded expression on my face.

No response from Jen, just wide eyes.

My body stiffened. Annoyed with her, I yelled, "My birthday's next week!"

She pulled a face. "Oh yeah," she said.

I couldn't tell if she knew it all along and was just messing with me, or if she'd totally missed it.

"And what is so notable about that day?" I asked, making sure she appreciated the full weight of it.

"You will turn thirteen and become a full-fledged teenager," she said, grinning big.

I mirrored her. "You're a genius."

Right away, we put a party plan into motion. Mom ordered a great big cake. It said, "Happy Birthday, Kat—Top Teen." We bought a variety of sodas and snacks—chips, dips, nuts, chocolate Kisses (my suggestion)—and added some left-over candy corn, which would probably become a staple of any party treats at our house for eternity.

Jen and I took care of the music. We put together a playlist on Spotify with a lineup of carefully selected songs arranged in a very particular order. Olivia Rodrigo's "good 4 u" was at the top. At the right moment, we would turn it on, allowing us to show off some of our hip-hoppity cheerleading moves from a knockoff version of the video we'd learned in our Just Dance class.

We bought loads of balloons, all colors, and stuffed party-favor bags with candy, all kinds. To save money, we made our own decorations and games. We drew up "Would She Rather?" sheets, where guests circled their choices—pizza or tacos, movies or video games, and a bunch of others—to test how well they knew the birthday girl. We designed glitzy Teen Zone signs to dangle from streamers hung all around the room. We chopped construction paper into confetti to rain down at the end. Of course, the biggest frill that took the most time was a huge sparkly "OMG UR A TEENAGER" banner that stretched the length of the room. The sparkles ended up everywhere. Mom hated it. I loved it.

We made calculated plans about everything, leaving nothing to chance. We'd be in the living room. Mom and Dad would be hanging out in the kitchen. Max would be banished to his room, a full flight upstairs. The furniture would be pushed back. The food and drink tables would be set up. We'd be ready.

It was a fantabulous plan!

Soon, everything in my life would change.

I would become a teenager with all of the recognition and privileges of teenhood. The prize I had ached for was in sight.

In anticipation of my big day, I discarded the letter *W* from my bulletin board. That's right. The TWEEN poster board was now prepped to officially become a TEEN board. The first posting would be a montage of photos from the party. What would hit the board next? Only a thirteen-year-old could know that.

Chapter 33

One of the biggest shockers of my life came before my birthday party when my parents did an about-face.

Mom and Dad had struggled to build up the gym business for so long that it seemed like the only thing they ever thought about. Well, now gym enrollment shot up practically overnight after Max and I helped save the day by bringing down the bad guy at the 7-Eleven and ending the crime spree in our neighborhood. Mom and Dad felt like they were sitting on top of the world, and they were rethinking a few things.

"This whole 7-Eleven disaster has been a wake-up call," Mom said. She launched into a pretty long spiel about how they'd been heaping a lot of responsibility on me for a long time and how I'd been a good soldier. She ended up saying, "Things are going to change."

I raised my eyebrows into question marks. I had no idea what she meant. All kinds of crazy stuff rolled through my head. Maybe they wanted to strike while the iron was hot, expand the gym or open another one. Maybe they wanted me to take over full-time parenting duties while they built up their business. *Oh no.* Maybe they wanted me to drop out of school, give up Will, run one of the gyms, and adopt Max. But that would be going a bit too far, even for them.

I shifted my focus back to my parents. "What things are going to change?"

Dad smiled and explained that the uptick in clients at the gym would mean more money for the family.

Money? I hesitated. Then I went for it. "Can we maybe buy me a new iPhone?"

"Sure," he said, like it wasn't even that big of a deal anymore. "I trust you to take care of it. And with your busy teenage schedule, I think you're going to need a more grown-up phone."

"Yes!" I pumped my fist in the air.

I figured this was the biggest victory to be scored until Mom said, "We can do more than that. We can hire some outside help—a bookkeeper at work or a babysitter at home." She lowered her glasses—a good sign this time—and winked at me. "After all, you are about to become a teenager, and you have a boyfriend. Maybe you'll even get a job this summer."

I couldn't believe it. They were treating me like a real teenager with a life. Just a few months ago, my parents had been scouting for second jobs, and my mom had labeled me a "child" after my performance at the talent show. Of course, business had picked up at the gym. And I had braved some tough showdowns and coped with some mind-changing moments of truth. It was time for me to be a teenager and for everyone else to treat me like one.

"For reals?" I asked.

"For real," Dad said.

I turned to Mom.

"Absolutely for real."

I hugged my dad. Then I hugged my mom, so tight that you could hardly tell where she left off and I began. I blinked back tears, and I had to admit I kind of lost it there for a sec. A tear even trickled down my cheek, but it was the very best kind.

My head was spinning with the good news. I could barely believe this wild turn of events that was seriously too good to be true. I waited for the catch. But it never came.

Chapter 34

Party day was here! I was excited and nervous all at once.

Jen came over to help with the setup. We tied up colorful balloons. We taped "Would She Rather?" sheets to the walls. We lined up party favors. Then we strung our extra glittery, monster-sized "OMG UR A TEENAGER" banner across the living room. We stepped back and admired it. The millions of sparkles shimmered, announcing the leap of Kat Cruz from tween to teen. *Excellent!*

We radiated confidence as we prepped for the party. Jen was wearing a sequined sweatshirt and a denim miniskirt. I made my entrance in a cotton-candy-pink midriff-flaunting crop top and ripped skinny jeans. Jen's red pixie was gelled for maximum style, and my black mane was curled and cascaded down to my shoulders. Even though the right half of my head was shaved, it was starting to grow in, and I was digging the edgy look.

Things started out kind of low-key. My party guests showed up mostly on time. Will looked so handsome in his black T-shirt and jeans. Some of the guests filled out the "Would She Rather?" sheets and giggled. Mostly, boys lumped with boys and girls with girls. Each group appeared totally self-absorbed, though I would catch a girl here or a boy there at almost any given moment sneaking a peek at the other camp. It was time to bring them together, and Jen and I would do the honors.

We placed fourteen candles on the cake—thirteen plus one to grow on—and coaxed all fourteen boys and girls closer for the celebration. We had the standard singing of the song, *Happy B-day, blah, blah, blah,* followed by the usual serving of ice cream and cake. Then we cranked up the volume for our "good 4 u" dance that drew applause and some copycat performances.

I grabbed Will, Jen pulled over James, and we encouraged the copycats to do the same. It wasn't long before almost everyone was taking their cue from us and dancing to the music.

But before we lost the high-spirited momentum and kids started to drift apart, we flipped on the more mellow sounds—the ones that whispered, *Let's snuggle closer.* It was all perfect. Except for Will. He got a sort of weirded-out zombie look on his face.

What could be wrong? Did I have a disgusting zit on the tip of my nose? Slimy green stuff stuck between my teeth? Were offensive beads of sweat forming on my upper lip?

That was what was going on inside my hot head. But on the outside, I played it frosty. "Everything cool with you?" I asked, free and easy as I could.

"Yup." He paused. "Everything's great with me." He shifted his weight from foot to foot.

"So, why're you looking at me like I have three eyeballs?"

He ran his hand through his sandy curls of hair. "I'm gonna tell you something." Another awkward pause.

My stomach was squeezing into knots. "What is it?" I asked.

Will looked sheepish. "Let's go upstairs," he said.

I felt dizzy. I almost fell over. Did he want to go to my room? That had happened in one of my magical daydreams about life as a teenager, but not in my real life. I wasn't sure I was ready to go upstairs.

Still, when he steered me toward the steps, I followed. My heart was in my mouth. "Yeah, let's go," I muttered.

Alone with Will. My brain was running wild. *What would he want to talk about?* My body tingled all over with such thoughts. What would he think about my room? I suddenly felt self-conscious about the TEEN board and the stupid stuffed animals on my bed. He was going to think I was such a baby.

At the top of the steps, I smiled longingly at him. He was awesome, and for a short sec I had this vision of us walking off into the sunset together. I could almost hear violins playing in the background.

"Now can you tell me?" I asked softly.

"Yes," he whispered. "There is blood—not too much—on the back of your jeans."

I gulped and swallowed hard. I swiveled my head around for a quick look. When I turned back, my eyes fixed in a dazed stare on Will. I wanted the earth to open and swallow me up.

SHOOT ME NOW. PLEASE!

I raced to my room, pulled out a Kotex pad I had stashed there, grabbed some fresh panties and jeans, rushed to the bathroom, tore off my clothes, cleaned up, and placed the pad in my underwear. I ran back to my room, threw on some pajamas, and burst into racking sobs.

———————

I was still sniffling and dabbing at my unstoppable tears when I heard a knock on my door.

"Honey, it's Mom."

"Come in," I said in a voice so low even I could barely hear it.

She sank down next to me on the edge of my bed. "What happened?"

"My period," I moaned. "Will saw it."

"Oh," she said with a slow nod of her head.

"My life sucks," I whimpered, wiping away more tears with a tissue that was in shreds.

"It's not so bad," she said, handing me another Kleenex.

"Not so bad?" I sat up to face her. "It's a

thousand times worse than bad. A bull's-eye was sitting on my butt, and I didn't even see it." I collapsed back into my pillows. "My stomach was cramping up and my head was swirling around. I thought I was just nervous."

"These things happen." Mom sighed. "You're growing up."

"But why did it have to happen now?" I fished for another tissue and sank even deeper into my bed.

Just then, there was another knock on the door. "What's going on?" Jen asked, slipping into the room.

"You know?" I whipped the sheet over my head and groaned.

"All I know is that Will told me to find you."

I yanked down the sheet. "Didn't he leave?"

"No. He's sitting in the living room."

I caught her up on my whole bloody-period episode and asked her to deliver a message. "Tell him to enjoy the party or go home because I'll probably never leave my room again." I sniffled and blew my nose.

Mom cocked her head to one side. "I don't think you'll be able to avoid everyone forever."

"Yeah, silly," Jen said. "Come back down to the party." She gave me two big thumbs-up.

I stared at them like they were out of their ever-lovin' minds. "No way." They could poke fun all they liked, but my days in the public eye were over. I folded my arms around my scrunched-up body and gazed off into the distance, pondering my empty life.

"Besides," I mumbled, "I can imagine all the trash talk flying around the room."

"No," Jen said. "I don't think anyone else knows."

I wrinkled my face at her.

"Really," she said, bobbing her head up and down.

I rolled out of my slouch and fidgeted with the edge of the sheet. I sat cross-legged with my hands on my knees. Then I slid my legs over the edge of my bed. But it was like I was made of lead and stuck there in limbo.

"My party life is over," I finally sighed and sank back on my bed of pain.

Dad knocked on my door and poked his head into the room. "Everyone coming out soon?"

Then Max shot through the doorway, dashed

over to me, and flung his arms around my neck, entangling me in his netting. "Kattie, you okay?"

"Not now, Spider-Man," I said, detangling myself and shoving him away.

"Kattie's fine, and we're all coming out right now," Mom said, herding Max out ahead of her.

For a split second, I thought how magical it would be if I could go back to my special birthday party and dance with Will one more time. But, of course, it was impossible.

"I'm not coming out!" I cried. I buried my head underneath my pillow until everyone was gone. Then I stayed in my room, throwing my own pity party, while Jen, Mom, and Dad wrapped up the party downstairs.

Chapter 35

The next morning, there was a light tapping at my door.

"Come in," I moaned.

Mom sailed into the room with a grin like sunshine. "I'm serving a special breakfast in bed to a very special grown-up lady," she said. It was freshly squeezed orange juice and a big slice of birthday cake left over from the party.

"Mom, you didn't have to do that," I said. But I was happy she did. It even forced a faint smile onto my gloomy face.

"How's my little woman feeling today?" she asked in a cheery way.

"A tiny bit better," I pouted. "Older," I reflected. "Actually, I'm thrilled that my period *finally* came . . . and it wasn't awful . . . just the natural course of becoming a woman." A big grin lit up my face for the first time since the party.

"Wait. There's more," Mom said. She dashed over to the door and brought back a huge box gift wrapped with an enormous pink bow on the top. "Open it."

I slipped off the ribbon, ripped away the pink paper, and uncovered what looked like a lifetime supply of Kotex. I couldn't keep myself from laughing. "You shouldn't have," I said. Then both of us cracked up.

Dad came in next and announced that he had a special delivery.

"For me?"

"It has your name on it, and it was outside our front door." He placed it on my lap.

It was a simple white box, the kind you saw in bakeries, and like Dad said, it had my name on it. Inside was a giant cupcake with gobs of gooey orange frosting and pictures of a witch and a ghost on top. It was a supersized version of the cupcakes Will and I had shared at the Halloween party, where he'd compared me to the Good Witch of the North from the Land of Oz. *How sweet is that?* The attached note, like his others, didn't say much—To: Kat, From: Will—but it warmed everything inside of me.

"I guess he must like you," Dad said.

I blushed. I couldn't think of anything to say, but my smile was as wide as the Cheshire cat's.

I texted Will a big "THANK YOU" with a smiley face.

Then Max pounded on my door. "Can I come in?"

"Why not?" I said.

He swooped in and propelled himself up onto the bed. He caught my juice in one of his spider webs, but I caught the glass mid-fall so it didn't cause a big mess.

"Sooorrry," he said with a long face.

"It's nothing," I said.

Moe followed Max into the room, and soon the whole family was hanging out on my bed, sharing bites of Will's generous cupcake and my Top Teen birthday cake. Crumbs were falling everywhere, but no one cared, not even Mom. And at that moment, soaking in all of my family's support and lovin' it, I thought, *I wouldn't disown a single member of my family for the world—not even pesky Max or slobbering Moe.*

That evening, Mrs. Morris sent Will over to collect a serving tray she'd loaned to us for the party. Mom had stacked it with some of her delicious homemade cookies.

Afterward, Will and I hung out on the porch. It was a good place for a private talk. The trouble was, neither one of us seemed to know how to start.

I ended up opening the convo with my usual sparkling, "Hey."

Will smiled. He shuffled his feet around, stuffed his hands in his pockets, and leaned back against the porch railing. "That was some party last night."

We exchanged a look.

"Unfortunately," I said, heaving a huge sigh, "it turned into a surprise party for me." I could only imagine what a gross-out it had been for Will.

I hugged my body and gazed up at the sky, hoping some clever chitchat would miraculously come to me. When it didn't, I flopped down into one of the big wooden porch chairs. Mom had placed those deep Adirondacks there when we moved in, saying they would be perfect for talking things over and working them out. They weren't inspiring me much, though.

I quit trying to think up something really bussin' to say and let the truth tumble out.

"I'm so embarrassed," I gushed with my

feelings splattering all over the place. Even I didn't see such an emotional outburst coming. What must Will have thought? Red-faced, I turned away from him.

Will stayed by me, waiting.

I finally half shrugged and faced him. "Thanks for getting me out of there."

"No worries," he said. He moved toward me, rested his hand gently on my shoulder, and spoke softly. "I was the only one who noticed. I want you to know that."

I lifted an eyebrow. "You mean you didn't tell your best buddy Chip anything about my *episode*?"

"I swear to God, no one knows."

"Thanks again, then," I said with a rush of genuine gratitude. "Really. Thanks."

"And all anyone will be talking about tomorrow will be the fun party at your place over the weekend."

He shuffled his feet around some more. Then he sank down into the chair beside me, and we were both quiet for a while. I plucked a piece of lint from my jeans. Will examined his shoelaces.

Eventually, he tossed me a side glance. "You know, you got everyone movin'." He wagged his head at me and chuckled. "I have to admit, I felt like a clumsy dork when you tugged me out on the dance floor."

We both laughed. The mood lightened and it was easier to just talk.

"Hey," I said, "we could work on that dance impediment thing you have going on."

"Yeah?" He tilted his head to one side.

I did the same back at him. "Yeah."

We were feeling a pretty good vibe and about to seal the deal with a high five when he just stopped all of a sudden. He wrinkled his forehead. Not even a trace of a smile line was left on his face. "There is a string attached," he said.

The smile slid right off my face. *Oh no*, I thought. *Is another top-of-the-world moment about to be shattered?*

"What string?" I asked.

"That at the end of the lessons, you go to a dance with me."

My jaw dropped straight to the floor. Date number two? *PINCH ME*. I was so happy, I thought I might cry. Instead, I said very casually, "Sure."

Then I immediately started chattering away about how we were going to have to spend a whole lot of time practicing together so we could show some real swag in our dance moves. "I'm a hero now. I have an image to uphold."

Will saluted. "I'm all in," he said, laughing.

———————

Okay, so my thirteenth birthday party was a bust, even with low expectations, and mine were high. And yes, I finally got my period, but at the worst time. No magical conversion like in movies or fairytales took place. I didn't feel like Sleeping Beauty awakening or Cinderella transforming. But I was only an immature twelve-year-old when I believed in those fantastical things.

Strangely, as a thirteen-year-old living in the real world, I got something better than any fairytale by a mile. I got the biggest cupcake I'd ever seen from Will and the unspoken revelation that I would most likely be his favorite Good Witch of the North forever. Not to mention, Date number two—coming soon. Maybe something only a teenager could really appreciate.

Chapter 36

My mom once said that the Morrises would come around, and they did. Now it seemed as if everyone had come to their senses: my parents, Max, and even Maria. But most of all, *me*. It wasn't like I was going to stop wishing on birthday candles or dreaming about Writer of the Year awards, but I was on the road to making stuff happen. I already had my first "Tales Out of School" column in the *Albuquerque Journal* newspaper in the pipeline.

Tonight, everything in my life was in sync. It was one for the geometry books, the sweet cherry of angles on top of my mind-blowing day.

Will's bedroom window and my window were catty-corner to each other. If I parted my curtains and squished over to the far side of my window at just the right angle, and if Will lifted his shade and leaned far back against his window frame at exactly the same time, we could see each other. I had drawn back my curtain and stared out my window about a zillion times before, and it had never happened.

But there he was, adorable as could be, staring back at me. I smiled and he smiled. I waved and he waved. And then he blew me an enchanted kiss and I blew him one back. Sappy, but I swear I could feel that kiss tingling on my lips and all the way down to my tippy toes. It was like my own Juliet and Romeo balcony scene.

OMG, I thought. *I really am a legit teenager with an actual boyfriend, and I have my first job as a journalist. So awesome!*

Just as I was having my moment, I glanced down and saw Max gazing up with devilment in his eyes, first at me and then at Will. He broke into a brand-new chant: "Kattie loves Will! Kattie loves Will!"

Funny, I wasn't even fazed by it. I didn't squirm or sweat or turn red. I laughed at his goofy teasing. I looked over at Will and he was laughing too. Max found no fun in it, stopped his chanting, and wandered off.

The stars winked down at us. My heart beat against my chest. It was all good. After all, it was true. *Kat loves Will.*

About the Author

Leslie Young has a BA degree in English from the University of Maryland and an MA degree in Comparative Literature from American University, where she also did graduate work in Journalism.

She has 25 years of experience teaching English in public schools and has worked as a TV news reporter for ABC affiliates and Capitol Hill news bureaus. She is a member of the SCBWI.

Young lives in Alexandria, Virginia.